If Simply Standing Beside Brian Could Make Tina Weak In The Knees, What Chance Did She Have To Keep Herself From Falling Back Into The *Stupid-With-Love* Category?

Focus. Tina wanted a baby.

And she wanted Brian to be its father.

She could do this. It had been five years. She wasn't in love anymore. She wasn't a kid, trusting in one special man to make her dreams come true.

She was mature enough to handle Brian without getting burned again. And if she was still breathlessly attracted to him, that was a good thing. It would make seducing him that much easier.

Brian looked confused. Also good. If she could just keep him off his guard for a week or two, things would work out fine.

But long after he'd gone inside his apartment, Tina was still looking out the window. And she couldn't help wondering which of them was really off their guard....

Dear Reader,

This May, Silhouette Desire's sensational lineup starts with Nalini Singh's *Awaken the Senses*. This DYNASTIES: THE ASHTONS title is a tale of sexual awakening starring one seductive Frenchman. (Can you say ooh-la-la?) Also for your enjoyment this month is the launch of Maureen Child's trilogy. The THREE-WAY WAGER series focuses on the Reilly brothers, triplets who bet each other they can stay celibate for ninety days. But wait until brother number one is reunited with *The Tempting Mrs. Reilly*.

Susan Crosby's BEHIND CLOSED DOORS series continues with *Heart of the Raven,* a gothic-toned story of a man whose self-imposed seclusion has cut him off from love…until a sultry woman, and a beautiful baby, open up his heart. Brenda Jackson is back this month with a new Westmoreland story, in *Jared's Counterfeit Fiancée,* the tale of a fake engagement that leads to real passion. Don't miss Cathleen Galitz's *Only Skin Deep,* a delightful transformation story in which a shy girl finally falls into bed with the man she's always dreamed about. And rounding out the month is *Bedroom Secrets* by Michelle Celmer, featuring a hero to die for.

Thanks for choosing Silhouette Desire, where we strive to bring you the best in smart, sensual romances. And in the months to come look for a new installment of our TEXAS CATTLEMAN'S CLUB continuity and a brand-new TANNERS OF TEXAS title from the incomparable Peggy Moreland.

Happy reading!

Melissa Jeglinski

Melissa Jeglinski
Senior Editor
Silhouette Books

Please address questions and book requests to:
Silhouette Reader Service
U.S.: 3010 Walden Ave., P.O. Box 1325, Buffalo, NY 14269
Canadian: P.O. Box 609, Fort Erie, Ont. L2A 5X3

The Tempting MRS. REILLY

MAUREEN CHILD

Silhouette® Desire

Published by Silhouette Books
America's Publisher of Contemporary Romance

SILHOUETTE BOOKS

ISBN 0-373-76652-1

THE TEMPTING MRS. REILLY

Visit Silhouette Books at www.eHarlequin.com

Printed in U.S.A.

Books by Maureen Child

Silhouette Desire

Have Bride, Need Groom #1059
*The Surprise Christmas
    Bride* #1112
Maternity Bride #1138
The Littlest Marine #1167
*The Non-Commissioned
    Baby* #1174
*The Oldest Living Married
    Virgin* #1180
Colonel Daddy #1211
Mom in Waiting #1234
Marine under the Mistletoe #1258
The Daddy Salute #1275
The Last Santini Virgin #1312
The Next Santini Bride #1317
Marooned with a Marine #1325
*Prince Charming in
    Dress Blues* #1366
His Baby! #1377
Last Virgin in California #1398
Did You Say Twins?! #1408
The SEAL's Surrender #1431
The Marine & the Debutante #1443
The Royal Treatment #1468
Kiss Me, Cowboy! #1490
Beauty & the Blue Angel #1514
Sleeping with the Boss #1534

Man Beneath the Uniform #1561
Lost in Sensation #1611
Society-Page Seduction #1639
†*The Tempting Mrs. Reilly* #1652

Harlequin Historicals

Shotgun Grooms #575
"Jackson's Mail-Order Bride"

Silhouette Books

Love Is Murder
"In Too Deep"

Summer in Savannah
"With a Twist"

Silhouette Special Edition

Forever...Again #1604

*Bachelor Battalion
†Three-Way Wager

MAUREEN CHILD

is a California native who loves to travel. Every chance they get, she and her husband are taking off on another research trip. The author of more than sixty books, Maureen loves a happy ending and still swears that she has the best job in the world. She lives in Southern California with her husband, two children and a golden retriever with delusions of grandeur.

Visit her Web site at www.maureenchild.com.

To Desire readers—

You guys are the best. The reason we do what we do. Thank you for your continued support!

Happy reading!

Maureen

One

"**T**en thousand bucks is a lot of money," Brian Reilly said and, grabbing his beer, leaned back against the scarred, red Naugahyde bench seat.

"Don't make plans," his brother Aidan added quickly as he snatched a tortilla chip from the wooden bowl set in the middle of the table. "You don't get it all, remember."

"Yeah," Connor added. "You have *us* to share it with."

"And *me*," Liam said with a smile, "to guide you."

"Don't I know it." Brian grinned at his brothers. Liam, the oldest by three years, looked completely at home, sitting in the dimly lit barroom. Not so unusual, unless you took into account the fact that Liam was a priest. But first and foremost, he was a Reilly. And the Reilly brothers were a unit. Now and always.

As the word *unit* shot through his brain, Brian turned his gaze on the other two men at the table with him. It was like looking into a mirror—twice. The Reilly triplets. Aidan, Brian and Connor. Named alphabetically in order of their appearances, the three of them had been standing together since the moment they took their first steps.

They'd even joined the Marine Corps together, doing their time in boot camp in stoic solidarity. They'd always been there for each other—to give moral support or a kick in the ass—whichever was required at the time.

Now, they were meeting to celebrate a windfall.

Their great-uncle Patrick, himself the last surviving brother of a set of triplets, had died, and having no other relations, he'd left ten thousand dollars to the Reilly triplets. Now all they had to do was figure out how to split the money.

"I say we split it *four* ways," Connor said, shooting Liam a glance. "Reilly's—all for one and one for all."

Liam grinned. "I'd like to say no thanks," he admitted. "But, since the church really needs a new roof, I'll just say, I like how Connor thinks."

"Twenty-five hundred won't buy you a new roof,"

Aidan said. "Won't buy much of anything for any of us, really."

"I've been thinking about that, too," Liam said and looked at each of his brothers. "Why not have a contest? Winner take all?"

Brian felt the zing of competition and knew his brothers felt it, too. Nothing they liked better than competing. Especially against each other. But the quiet smile on Liam's face warned him that he wasn't going to like what was coming next. Sure, Liam was a priest, but being a Reilly first, made him tricky. "What kind of contest?" Brian asked.

Liam smiled. "Worried?"

"Hell no," Aidan put in. "The day a Reilly backs off a challenge is the day when—"

"—when he's six feet under," Connor finished for him. "What've you got in mind, Liam?"

Their older brother smiled again. "You guys are always talking about commitment and sacrifice, right?"

Brian glanced at his brothers before nodding. "Hell yes. We're Marines. We're all about sacrifice. Commitment."

"Ooh-rah!" Connor and Aidan hooted and high-fived each other.

"Yeah?" Liam leaned back and shifted his gaze between the three other men at the table. "But the fact is, you guys know zip about either."

Aidan and Connor blustered, but it was Brian who shut them up with a wave of his hand. *"Excuse me?"*

"Oh, I'm willing to acknowledge your military commitment. God knows I spend enough time praying for the three of you." His gaze drifted from one to the other of the triplets. "But this is something different. Harder."

"Harder than going into battle?" Connor took a sip of his beer and leaned back. "Please."

"Anything you can come up with, we can take," Aidan said.

"Damn straight," Brian added.

"Glad to hear it." Liam leaned his elbows on the tabletop and gazed from one triplet to the next as he lowered his voice. "Because this'll separate the Marines from the boys." He paused for effect, then said, "No sex for ninety days."

Silence dropped down on the table like a rock tossed from heaven.

"Come on," Connor said, shooting his siblings a look of wild panic.

"No way. Ninety *days*?" Aidan looked horrified.

Brian listened to the others, but kept his mouth shut, watching his older brother while he waited for the other shoe to drop. He didn't have long.

"I'm only talking about three months," Liam said, that wily smile on his face again. "Too hard for you guys? I've made that commitment for *life*."

Aidan shuddered.

"That's nuts." Connor shook his head.

"What's the matter?" Liam challenged. "Too scared to try?"

"Who the hell *wants* to try?" Aidan added.

"Three months with no sex? Impossible." Brian glared at Liam.

"You're probably right," the oldest brother said and smiled as he took another long drink of beer. Setting the bottle down onto the tabletop, he cradled it between his palms and said with a shrug, "You'd never make it anyway. None of you. Women have been after you guys since junior high. No way could you last three months."

"Didn't say we couldn't," Connor muttered.

"Didn't say we *would,* either," Aidan pointed out, just so no one would misunderstand.

"Sure, I understand," Liam said, shooting each of them a look. "What you're saying is, that clearly, a priest is way tougher than *any* Marine."

There was no way they were going to be able to live with *that* statement. In a matter of a few seconds, Liam had his deal and the triplets had signed on to the biggest challenge of their lives.

How they'd been sucked into the rest of it, Brian wasn't able to figure out, even days later. But he was pretty sure that Liam had missed his calling. He should have been a car salesman, not a priest.

"No sex for ninety days," Brian said, his gaze shifting to each of his brothers in turn. The other two Reilly triplets didn't look any happier about this than he did. But damned if he could see a way out of it without the three of them coming off looking like wusses. "Loser forfeits his share to the whole."

"And if you *all* lose," Liam added cheerfully, "my church gets the money for a new roof."

"We won't lose," Brian assured him. Not that he was looking forward to a short spate of celibacy, but now that he was in the competition, he was in it to win. Reillys didn't lose well.

"Glad to hear it," Liam said. "Then you won't mind the penalty phase."

"What penalty?" Brian eyed his older brother warily.

Liam grinned.

"You've been planning this, haven't you?" Connor demanded, leaning his forearms on the table.

"Let's say I've given it some thought."

"Quite a bit, obviously," Aidan mused.

Liam nodded. "The church *does* need a new roof, remember."

"Uh-huh." Brian glared at him. "But this isn't just about a roof, is it? This is about torturing *us*."

"Hey," Liam said with a crooked grin. "I'm the oldest. That's my job."

"Always were damn good at it," Connor murmured.

"Thank you. Now," Liam said, enjoying himself far too much, "onto the penalty phase. And I'm especially proud of this, by the way. Remember last year, when Captain Gallagher lost that round of golf to Aidan?"

Aidan grinned in fond memory, but Brian's brain jumped ahead, and realized just where Liam was going with this. "No way."

"Oh yeah. Gallagher looked so good in his costume, I figure it's perfect for you guys, too. Losers have to wear coconut bras and hula skirts while riding around the base in a convertible," Liam said, then added, "on Battle Color day."

The one day of the year when every dignitary, high-ranking officer and all of their families was on base for ceremonies. Oh yeah. The humiliation would be complete.

Aidan and Connor started arguing instantly, but Brian just watched Liam. When the other two wound down, he said, "Okay, big brother, what's *your* stake in this? I don't see you risking anything, here."

"Ah, I'm risking that new roof." Liam picked up his beer again, took another long swallow, then looked at each of his brothers. "My twenty-five hundred is riding on this, too. If one of you guys lasts the *whole* three months, then he gets all the money. If you *all* fold, which I suspect is going to happen, then the church gets it all, and the new roof is mine. Ours." He frowned. "The church's."

"And how do you know if we last the three months or not?"

"I'll take your word for it." Liam grinned. "You're a Reilly. We never lie. At least not to each other."

Brian looked at the mirror images of himself. He got brief, reluctant nods from each of them. Then he turned back to Liam. "You've got a deal. When does the challenge start?"

"Tonight."

"Hey, I've got a date with Deb Hannigan tonight," Connor complained.

"I'm sure she'll appreciate you being a gentleman," Liam said, smiling.

"This is gonna suck," Aidan said tightly.

Brian admitted silently, that Aidan had never been more right. Then he shifted his gaze to each of his brothers and wondered just which of them would be the last Reilly standing.

He fully intended that it would be *him*.

Tina Coretti Reilly parked her rental car in her grandmother's driveway, then opened the door and stepped out into the swampy heat of a South Carolina early-summer day.

She instantly felt as though she'd been smacked with a wet, electric blanket. Even in June, the air was thick and heavy, and she knew that by the end of August everyone in town would be praying for cooler weather.

Tiny Baywater, South Carolina, was barely more than a spot on the road outside Beaufort. Ancient, gnarled trees, magnolia, pine and oak, lined the residential streets, and Main Street, where dozens of small businesses hugged the curbs, was the hub of social activity. In Baywater, time seemed to move slower than anywhere else in the South, and that was saying something.

And Tina had missed it all desperately.

She stared up at the wide front porch of the old bungalow and memories rose up inside her so quickly, she nearly choked on them. She'd grown up in this house, raised by her grandmother, after her parents' death in a car accident.

From the time she was ten years old until five years ago, Baywater had been home. And in her heart, it still was, despite the fact that she now lived on the other side of the country. But California was far away at the moment.

Not far enough away though to block the memory of the conversation she'd had only yesterday.

"Are you insane?"

Tina laughed at her friend Janet's astonished expression. She couldn't really blame her. Janet had, after all, been the one to listen whenever Tina complained about her ex-husband.

"*Not legally,*" *Tina quipped.*

"*You are nuts. You're volunteering to go back to South Carolina, for God's sake, in the middle of summer, when the heat'll probably kill you, not to mention the fact that your ex is there.*"

"*That's the main reason I'm going, remember?*"

"*Yeah,*" *Janet said, easing her six-months pregnant bulk down until she could sit on the edge of her friend's desk. "I just don't think you've thought this all through.*"

"*Sure I have.*" *Tina sounded confident. She only wished she were. But if she stopped to think about this anymore, she just might change her mind and she didn't want to.*

At twenty-nine years of age, she could hear her biological clock ticking with every breath she took. And it wasn't getting quieter.

"*Look,*" *she said, staring up into Janet's worried brown gaze, "I know what I'm doing. Honest.*"

Janet shook her head. "I'm just worried," she admitted, running the flat of her hand across her swollen belly with a loving caress.

Tina's gaze dropped to follow the motion and she swallowed back a sigh that was becoming all too familiar lately. She wanted kids. She'd always wanted kids. And if she was going to do something about it, then it was time to get serious. "I know you're worried, but you don't have to be."

"Tina, I didn't meet you until six months after your divorce," Janet reminded her. *"And you were still torn up about it. Now, five years later, you still carry his picture in your wallet."*

Tina winced. *"Okay, but it is a great picture."*

"Granted," Janet agreed. *"But what makes you think you can let him back into your life and not suffer again?"*

A nugget of hesitation settled in the pit of Tina's stomach, but she ignored it. *"I'm not letting him into my life again. I'm dropping into his life. Then I'm going to drop out again."*

Janet sighed and stood up. *"Fine. I can't talk you out of this. But you'd better call me. A lot."*

"I will. Don't worry."

Of course, Janet would worry, Tina told herself as she came back from the memory. If she wasn't so determined on her own course, maybe she would be worrying, too. Her gaze slid from the front porch to the driveway and the garage and the apartment over that garage.

Maybe, she told herself, Janet was right. Maybe this was a mistake.

But at least she was doing *something*. For the past five years, she'd felt as though she'd been standing still. Sure, her career was terrific and she had good friends and a nice house. But she didn't have someone to love. And she needed that. Now, whether she was making the wrong move or not, at least she was *moving*.

That had to count for something.

"Of course," she muttered, tearing her gaze from the apartment, "you're not moving at the moment. And you've only got three weeks, Coretti—so don't waste time."

Grabbing her luggage from the trunk, she pulled up the handle and rolled the heavy case along the bumpy brick walk leading to the front door. The suitcase thumped against the four wooden steps and the wheels growled against the wide planked front porch.

When she unlocked the front door and stepped inside, Tina stopped in the foyer. The big front room was bright with sunshine streaming through the picture window. The air was cool, thanks to the air-conditioning her grandmother insisted on running even when she wasn't home and a vase full of lemon-yellow roses scented the room. It was just as she remembered and for a moment or two, Tina just stood there, enjoying the sensation of being home again.

Until the frantic barks and yips cut into her thoughts and reminded her that she wasn't entirely alone.

Closing the front door, she abandoned her suitcase and walked through the living room, into the kitchen and straight back through the mudroom to the back door.

Here, the noise was deafening. Tina chuckled as

she fumbled with the deadbolt. Thumps and scrapes against the outside of the door blended with more high-pitched barking that had the same effect as fingernails scraping across a blackboard.

In self-defense, she whipped open the back door and the noisemakers tumbled in, as though they'd been balanced against the door. Which they probably had been. Instantly, the two little white puffballs leaped at Tina. What felt like dozens of tiny feet with needlelike claws clambered over her legs and feet.

Muddy paw prints decorated the legs of her pale green linen slacks, looking like smudged black lace. The two little dogs tumbled over each other in their quest to be the first one petted. The sniffing and licking continued until Tina gave up trying to calm them down and fell to the floor laughing.

"Okay, you guys, I'm glad to see you, too." She tried to pet them but they wouldn't stand still long enough. And, as if sitting on her lap wasn't nearly good enough, both teacup poodles tried to dig their way inside her, squirming and pushing each other off Tina's lap.

Muffin and Peaches, one a pale cream color and the other, well, the color of ripe peaches. Nana's unimaginatively named, unclipped poodles were nuts about women and hated men. Which, Tina thought, put them pretty much in the same boat with a lot of Tina's friends.

Tina on the other hand, didn't hate men.

She didn't even hate the one man she should have.

In fact, that one man was the real reason she'd come back to Baywater.

Oh, Nana had asked her to stay at the house and take care of "her girls" while the older woman and two of her friends were taking a tour of Northern Italy. But the timing of Nana's trip and Tina's private epiphany seemed destined by fate. It was as if the universe had grabbed Tina, given her a shake and said *Here you go, girl. Go get what you want.*

Because as happy as Tina was to do Nana a favor, there'd been another, more important reason for agreeing to come home for two weeks.

She wanted to get pregnant.

And the man she needed to get the job done was living here, over the garage.

Her ex-husband.

Brian Reilly.

Two

The two spoiled mutts sent up a racket the minute Brian pulled into the driveway. Scowling, he shut the engine off and shot a grim look toward the backyard where the little bastards were probably trying to scratch through the gate to get at him.

Shaking his head, he climbed out of the car and wondered again why the little dogs hated him. Maybe in a past life he'd been a dogcatcher or something and they could still smell it on him.

"Knock it off, you guys," he bellowed, not expecting his shout to do a thing about shutting them up. And he wasn't disappointed. If anything, the noise level climbed and the frantic urgency in their yips and high-pitched barks escalated.

One downside to living in the garage apartment at Angelina Coretti's house was putting up with those dogs. But, it was the *only* downside as far as Brian was concerned.

Renting that small, one-bedroom apartment worked out well for both him and Angelina. The older woman liked having him around—knowing he was handy if she needed help. And he had privacy, no worries about losing his apartment when he was deployed for months at a time, and a sweet old lady who enjoyed cooking, to make him the occasional home-cooked dinner.

On the whole, a situation worth putting up with Muffin and Peaches.

And there was another good point to his living arrangements. Since Angelina was his ex-wife's grandmother, Brian could keep a tenuous connection to Tina Coretti Reilly. It wasn't much, and probably wasn't real healthy, but Tina, even though they'd been divorced for five years now, was never too far out of his thoughts.

The barking got sharper, louder, as he stalked up the driveway toward the stairs at the side of the garage. Brian tossed another scowl at the whitewashed wooden gate and the hell hounds beyond. Then the back door opened and that scowl froze on his face.

It was as if all the air had been sucked from his lungs. His guts twisted and a hard ball of something hot and needy and just a little pissed landed in the pit of his stomach.

"Judging by that expression," Tina said, over the din of the dogs, "you're not real happy to see me."

Afternoon sunlight lit her up as brightly as if she'd been an actress standing at center stage. Her wide brown eyes danced with amusement. Her long, thick black hair hung down around her shoulders. She wore a pale green tank top that bared her tanned arms and chest, and he was only grateful that the gate was there, minimizing his view of her. He wasn't at all sure he'd be able to take seeing miles of long, tanned leg.

"Tina." He swallowed hard and cleared his throat. Damn it, if he was shaken to find her standing practically on top of him, he wouldn't let her see it. "What're you doing here?"

"I'm here to take care of the girls while Nana's in Italy."

The girls being Muffin and Peaches.

"Angelina didn't tell me you were coming."

"Any reason why she should?"

His eyes narrowed as he watched her. "Any reason why she shouldn't?"

"Ah," Tina said smiling, as she let the back door swing closed behind her. "Same ol' Brian. Answer a question with a question. Stall for time."

The dogs kept barking and he and Tina were shouting at each other just to be heard. His head was buzzing, brain racing. And he didn't want to think about the jolt his heart had just gotten. Damn it.

Angelina should have warned him.

Should have given him the chance to get the hell outta Dodge.

And, he admitted silently, since Angelina knew him well enough to know that he *would* have left, that's probably exactly why she hadn't told him about Tina's visit. The older woman had never made it a secret that she thought the two of them still belonged together. It would be just like Angelina to try for a little long distance matchmaking.

Too late to do anything about it now, anyway, Brian thought and told himself to get a grip. It wasn't easy.

Tina took the steps down from the back porch, opened the gate and the minute she did, the two little fleabags were on him. Stalking and pouncing as though they were the size of wolves instead of especially hairy rats, they attacked the laces of his tennis shoes and grabbed at the hem of his jeans. He glanced down at them, almost grateful for the distraction. "Cut it out."

"They really *don't* like you, do they?" Tina mused. "I mean, Nana told me they weren't very fond of you, but I figured she was exaggerating."

Brian heard her, but he wasn't listening. Instead, he

was watching her and wishing to hell she'd stayed behind the safety of that gate. It was just as he'd thought. She was wearing denim shorts that hugged her hips and displayed way too much smooth, tanned leg.

Blood pumped and rushed to the one spot in his body that had always responded to Tina. From their first date, the attraction between them had been electrical. And time hadn't changed a damn thing.

Which just made his black mood even blacker.

It had been two solid weeks since he'd made that stupid bet with his brothers. Two full weeks of no sex and he was already a man on the edge. By the end of three months, he'd be a gibbering idiot. And Tina's presence wasn't going to help anything.

"Damn it, Angelina should have warned me you were coming."

She stiffened slightly and lifted her chin in a defiant, *I'm ready to rumble* pose he remembered all too well. Damn. Their fights had been almost as good as the sex. And the sex had always been incredible.

"I asked her not to tell you."

"Why in the hell would you do that?" he demanded, and kicked his foot, trying to dislodge Peaches from his ankle. It didn't work. She managed to hang on.

"Because I knew if she told you that you'd find a way to disappear."

That rankled a little, but only because she was right. He would have signed on for extra duty, pleaded for a top-secret mission, asked to be deployed to a base several thousand miles away.

When, Brian suddenly wondered, had he become a coward about Tina?

Then he dismissed the question, because it wasn't relevant at the moment.

"Why would I do that?"

"I don't know, Brian," she said and cocked one hip as she folded both arms across her chest.

Well, *under* her breasts, pushing them higher, giving him a closer look at the smooth, tanned curve of flesh peeking up from the top of her low-cut shirt. He forced himself to lift his gaze to meet hers.

"But," she continued, keeping her gaze locked with his, "you always do. Every time I've visited Nana in the past couple of years, you've 'coincidentally' been called away."

Nothing coincidental about it. Ever since the divorce, he'd purposely avoided running into Tina. He reached up and shoved one hand across the side of his head. "I just wanted to make it easier on you. Visiting family without having to—"

"—see the man who divorced me without an explanation?" she finished for him.

She was still mad. Easy enough to see in the sparks shooting out of her dark brown eyes. He couldn't really blame her, either. "Look, Tina…"

"Forget it." She waved whatever he'd been about

to say away and shook her head until her hair whipped back behind her shoulders. "I didn't mean to start anything. I just wanted to see you. That's all."

Brian studied her and wished to hell he could read her mind. Dealing with Tina had never been easy, but it had always been an adventure. And if he knew her, then there was something else going on besides just wanting to say hi to her ex.

Still, he told himself, *did* he know her anymore? They'd been married for one year and divorced for five. So maybe he didn't. Maybe she'd changed. Become a stranger. The thought of which left him a lot colder than it should have.

"Why'd you want to see me?" His eyes narrowed suspiciously.

Her eyes went wide and innocent. "Jeez, Brian, lighten up. Can't an ex-wife say hello without getting the third degree?"

"An ex-wife who flies in all the way from California to say hello?"

"And to take care of two sweet little—"

"—furry monsters," he finished for her and snarled at Peaches who was trying desperately to crawl up his leg. Probably wanted to bite through his jugular.

Tina laughed and everything inside him went still.

He looked at her from the corner of his eye and watched her like a hungry man eyes a steak. *Di-*

vorced, he reminded himself, but still just the sound of her laughter could reach down inside him and warm all the cold, empty spots.

Five years since the last time he'd touched her and his fingertips could *still* feel the softness of her skin. Her perfume, a soft blend of flowers and citrus, seemed always to be with him, especially in his dreams. And the memories of their lovemaking could make him groan with need.

Hell.

Especially now.

Man, he so didn't need Tina in town with this stupid bet going on.

"I don't know why they don't like you," Tina said as she bent down to scoop Muffin into the crook of her arm. The little dog quivered in excitement and affection and gave Tina's neck a couple of long swipes of its tongue.

Brian wouldn't mind doing the same.

He spoke up fast, to keep that image from coalescing. "Because they know it's mutual."

Tina scratched Muffin behind her ear, giving the dog a taste of heaven and giving herself something to do with her hands. If she hadn't picked up the dog, she might have given in to the urge to grab Brian. Her mouth watered just looking at him.

His black hair was still militarily short, showing

off the sharp angles and planes of his face to model perfection. His dark blue eyes were still as deep and mysterious as the ocean at night. His black USMC T-shirt strained over broad shoulders and a muscular chest and his narrow hips and long legs looked unbelievably good encased in worn denim.

She'd forgotten, God help her.

She'd forgotten just how much he could affect her.

Maybe Janet had been right. Maybe this wasn't such a good idea after all.

She wanted a baby, sure.

And she wanted Brian to be its father.

But if simply standing beside the man could make her weak in the knees, what chance did she have to keep herself from falling back into the *stupid-with-love* category?

As soon as that thought flitted through her mind though, she firmly pushed it aside. She could do this. It had been five years. She wasn't in love anymore. She wasn't a kid, trusting in one special man to make her dreams come true.

She'd worked long and hard at her career. She was respected. She was mature enough to handle Brian Reilly without getting her fingers burned again. And if she was still breathlessly attracted to him, that was a good thing.

It would make seducing him that much easier.

"Look, Brian," she said, keeping a tight grip on

Muffin while Peaches scrabbled at the hem of Brian's jeans again, "there's no reason we can't be civil to each other, is there?"

"I guess not."

"Good." It was a start, anyway. "So, I'm going to barbecue a steak tonight. Want me to add one for you?"

For one small second, she thought he was going to say yes. She could see it in his eyes. The hesitation. Then he apparently got over it.

"No, thanks. Gotta go see Connor tonight. He's uh…having some problems with his uh—"

Tina smiled and shook her head. "You never were much of a liar, Brian."

He stiffened. "Who's lying?"

"You are," she said, smiling. Then she turned for the gate leading to the backyard and the house. "But that's okay, I'm not taking it personally. Yet. Come on, Peaches. Dinner."

Instantly, the little dog released her hold on Brian and scuttled for the backyard and her food dish.

"Tina," Brian said.

She stopped at the gate and flashed him a smile. It was good to know she could still get to him so easily. If he hadn't been worried about being alone with her, he never would have lied about having to meet Connor.

And now, he looked…confused. Also good. If she could just keep him off his guard for a week or two, things would work out fine.

"It's okay, Brian," she said, giving him a shrug and a brighter smile. "I'm going to be here for almost three weeks. I'm sure we'll be seeing plenty of each other."

"Yeah." He shoved his hands into his jeans pockets and hunched his broad shoulders as if trying to find a way to balance a burden that had been dropped onto him without warning.

She wasn't sure she liked the analogy much, but it seemed to fit.

"Have a good night," she called out as she closed the gate behind her, "and say hi to Connor."

"Right."

Tina went into the house with the dogs, and once the back door was closed, she fingered the edge of the white Priscilla curtains until she could see the stairway leading to the garage apartment. Brian climbed those stairs like a man headed for the gallows.

And when he reached the landing, he paused and looked back at the house.

Tina flinched. It was almost as if his gaze had locked with hers instinctively. She felt the heat and power of that steady stare and it rocked her right to her bones.

Long after he'd gone inside his apartment, Tina was still standing in the kitchen, looking out the window. And she couldn't help wondering which of them was really off their guard.

* * *

Two hours later, Brian was finishing dinner and listening to Connor laugh at the latest development. It was his own fault. Not that he'd been expecting sympathy, but outright hilarity was a little uncalled for.

"So, Tina's back in town," Connor said, grinning. "Man, I can almost feel that money sliding into my wallet as we speak."

"Forget it," Brian snapped, still feeling the effects of Tina's smile hours later. "She's not going to help you win this bet. *I* divorced *her*, remember?"

"Yeah," Connor said and signaled to the waiter for another beer. "Never did understand why, though."

None of his family had understood, Brian thought, momentarily allowing himself to drift down memory lane. Hell, even *he'd* had a hard time coming to grips with the fact that divorcing Tina had been the only right thing to do.

It hadn't been easy. But it had been right.

He still believed that.

If he didn't, he wouldn't be able to live with the regrets.

Tina Coretti still haunted him. At the oddest times, his brain would suddenly erupt into images of her. Cooking, laughing, singing off-key with the radio while on one of their notorious road trips. He remembered arguing with her, both of them shouting until one of them started laughing and then how they'd tumble into bed and rediscover each other.

The sex had always been amazing between them.

Not just bodies coming together, but in his more poetic moments, Brian had convinced himself that even their souls had mated.

And once she was gone from his life, he'd had to believe it, because he'd been left hollow. Empty. His heart broken and his soul crushed, despite knowing that what he'd done, he'd done for *her.*

That hadn't changed.

He shoved what was left of his burger and fries to the edge of the table for the waiter to pick up, then leaned back in his seat.

The Lighthouse Restaurant was packed, as it generally was. Families crowded around big tables and couples snuggled close together in darkened booths. Overhead, light fell from iron chandeliers bristling with hanging ferns and copper pots.

Studying his brother across the table from him, Brian shifted the talk from himself by asking suddenly, "So how're *you* doing on the bet front?"

Connor choked on a swallow of beer and when he was finished coughing, he shook his head. "Man, it's way uglier than I thought it was going to be."

Brian laughed.

"Seriously," Connor protested. "Getting to the point where I'm hiding from women completely."

"I know what you mean," Brian said, though for him, hiding had just gotten a lot harder. Staying away from women at work was easy. There weren't that many female pilots or female personnel assigned to the F-18 squadrons. And those that were there made a point of avoiding the *guys*. Couldn't blame them. They had to work twice as hard as the men just to be accepted and they weren't going to blow a career by flirting with their fellow officers.

So work was safe and Brian had planned to hide out at home, staying away from the usual spots, bars, clubs and whatever, to avoid women in his off-duty hours. But now, home wasn't a refuge. Instead, with Tina in town, home was the most dangerous territory of all.

"It's only been two weeks," Connor admitted, "and already, I've got way more respect for Liam."

"I'm with you there," Brian said.

"Talked to Aidan last night and he says he's thinking about joining a monastery for three months."

The thought of that was worth a chuckle. "At least he's suffering, too."

"Yeah." Connor narrowed his eyes, nodded at the waiter, who stopped by to deliver their check, then said, "At least I get to take out my frustrations by screaming at the 'boots' every day."

Brian smiled but couldn't help feeling sorry for the new recruits under Connor's charge in boot camp.

Then his brother spoke up again.

"Have you noticed the only one who's *not* suffering is our brother the priest?" Clearly disgusted, Connor shook his head. "He's just sitting back laughing at the three of us. How'd he talk us into this, anyway?"

"He let us talk ourselves into it. None of us could ever resist a challenge. Or a dare."

"We're that predictable?"

"To him anyway. Remember, priest or not," Brian said, "he's still the sneakiest of us."

"Got that right." Connor reached for his wallet and pulled out a couple of bills, tossing them onto the tabletop. "So, what're you gonna do about Tina?"

"I'm gonna stay as far away from her as I can, that's what."

"That was never easy for you."

Brian tossed his money down, too, then grumbled, "Didn't say it was gonna be easy."

Connor stood up, looked at his brother and gave him a smile. "We could try the old switcheroo trick. Since you have a hard time being around her, I could talk to her. Ask her to leave."

Brian looked at him and slowly slid out of the booth. They hadn't used the switcheroo since they were kids. The triplets were so identical, even their mother had sometimes had a hard time keeping them straight. So, the three of them had often used that confusion to their advantage, with one of them pre-

tending to be the other in order to get out of something they didn't want to do. They'd fooled teachers,
coaches and even, on occasion, their own mother
and father.

But, Brian reminded himself, as the idea began to
appeal to him, Tina had always been able to tell them
apart. They'd never once fooled her as they had so
many others. Still, he thought, watching Connor
smile and nod encouragingly, it had been *years* since
she'd seen the three Reilly brothers together. *Years*
since Tina and Brian were close enough that she'd
been able to pick him out of a crowd of three with
pure instinct.

"I'm willing if you want to give it a shot," Connor prodded.

What did he have to lose? Brian asked himself. If
Tina didn't catch on to the trick, maybe she would
leave, making Brian's life a little easier. And if she
did catch on…well, it had been a long time since he'd
seen Tina Coretti's temper.

And as he remembered it, she looked damn good
when she was fighting mad.

Three

Tina heard Brian's car when he returned to the house late that night and she breathed a quiet sigh of relief. Moving to the curtains of the upstairs bedroom that had been hers since she was a child, she peeked out to watch him walk up the driveway. When he paused long enough to snarl insults at the barking dogs, she smiled.

She'd been half worried that he might bolt. It would have been easy for him to up and move to the base for a few weeks just to avoid her. But he hadn't. And she was pretty sure she knew why.

Brian would never admit that he wasn't up to the challenge of seeing her every day. He'd never allow himself to acknowledge that there was anything to worry *about*.

He took the flight of steps to the garage apartment two at a time and her heartbeat quickened just watching him move. By the time he opened his door and went inside, without a glance at the house, her mouth was dry and her breath came in short fits and starts.

"Okay," she muttered, "maybe *I'm* the one who should be worried."

When the phone rang, she lunged for it gratefully. Sprawled across the hand-sewn quilt covering her double bed, Tina snatched at the "princess" style telephone and said, "Hello?"

"So, you're there."

"Janet." Tina rolled over onto her back and stared up at the beamed ceiling. Smiling, she said, "Right back where I started, yep."

"Have you seen him?"

"Oh yeah."

"And…?"

Tina grabbed the twisted cord in one hand and wrapped the coils around her index finger as she talked. "And, he's just like I remembered." Actually, he was *more* than she remembered. More handsome. More irresistible. More aggravating.

"So you're still set on this."

Tina sighed. "Janet, we've been all through this. I don't want to go to a sperm bank. Can you imagine *that* conversation with my child? 'Yes, honey, of course you have a daddy. He's number 3075. It's a very *nice* number.'"

Janet laughed. "Fine. I'm just saying, it seems like you're asking for trouble here. I'm worried."

"And I appreciate it." Tina smiled and let her gaze drift around her old bedroom. Nana hadn't changed much over the years. There were still posters of Tahiti and London tacked to the walls, bookcases stuffed with books and treasures from her teenage years and furniture that had been in the Coretti family since the beginning of time.

There was comfort here.

And Tina was surprised to admit just how much she needed that comfort.

Though she'd been born and raised in this house, this town, she'd been gone a long time. And stepping into the past, however briefly, was just a little unnerving.

"But you want me to back off," Janet said.

Tina heard the smile in her friend's voice. "Yeah, I do."

"Tony told me you'd say that," Janet admitted, then shouted to her husband, "okay, okay. I owe you five dollars."

Tina laughed and felt the knots in her stomach slowly unwinding. "I'm glad you called."

"Yeah?"

"Yeah. I needed to hear a friendly voice," Tina admitted. With Nana in Italy and Brian holed up in his cave, Tina had been feeling more alone than she had in a long time. "Even I didn't know how much I needed it."

"Happy to help," Janet said. "Call me if you need to talk or cry or shout or…anything."

"I will. And I'll see you in three weeks."

After her friend hung up, Tina sat up and folded her legs beneath her. She looked around her room and felt the past rise up all around her. She'd still been living in this room when she and Brian had started dating.

It felt like a lifetime ago.

Back then, she was still working part-time at Diego's, an upscale bar on the waterfront, and studying for her MBA during the day. Brian was a lieutenant, the pilot's wings pinned to his uniform still shiny and new. He'd walked into the bar one night, and just like the corniest of clichés, their eyes met, flames erupted and that was that.

In a rush of lust and love, they'd spent every minute together for the next month, then infuriated both of their families with a hurried elopement. But they'd been too crazy about each other to wait for the big, planned, fancy wedding their families would have wanted.

Instead, it was just the two of them, standing in front of a justice of the peace. Tina had carried a single rose that Brian had picked for her from the garden out in front of the courthouse. And she'd known, deep in her bones, that this man was her soul mate. The one man in the world that she'd been destined to love.

They'd had one year together. Then Brian dropped the divorce bomb on her and left the next morning for a six-month deployment to an aircraft carrier.

"So much for soul mates," Tina whispered to the empty room as she left the memories in her dusty past where they belonged. Then she flopped back onto the bed, threw one arm across her eyes and tried to tell herself that the ache in her heart was just an echo of old pain.

The next day, Tina dived into work on her grandmother's garden. Nana loved having flowers, but she wasn't keen on weeding. She always claimed that it was because she had no trouble getting down onto the grass, but getting back up was tougher. But Tina knew the truth. Her grandmother just hated weeding. Always had.

The roses were droopy, the Gerbera daisies were being choked out by the dandelions and the pansies had given up the ghost. Tina knelt in the sun-warmed grass and let the summer heat bake into her skin as she leaned into the task.

Classic rock played on the stereo in the living

room and drifted through the open windows to give her a solid beat to work to. The sounds of kids playing basketball and a dog's frantic bark came from down the street. Muffin and Peaches watched Tina's every move from behind the screen door and yipped excitedly whenever something interesting, like a butterfly, passed in their line of vision.

She'd already been at it for an hour when she straightened up, put her hands at the small of her back and stretched, easing the kinks out of muscles unused to gardening. In California, Tina lived in an apartment and made do with a few potted plants on the balcony overlooking Manhattan Beach. At home, she was always too busy working, or thinking about working, or planning to be working, to do anything else. And when had that happened? she asked herself. When had she lost her sense of balance? When had work become more important than living?

But she knew the answer.

It seemed as though everything in her life boiled back down to Brian. She'd buried herself in her ambition when he'd divorced her. As if by immersing herself in work she could forget about the loneliness haunting her. It hadn't worked.

It felt good to be out in a yard again, she thought. Good to not be watching a clock or worrying about a lunch meeting. It was good just to *be,* even if the

South Carolina humidity was thick enough to slice with a knife.

A thunderous, window rattling roar rose up out of nowhere suddenly and Tina tipped her head back in time to see an F-18 streak across the sky, leaving a long white trail behind it. Her heart swelled as it always did when she spotted a military jet. Every time, she imagined that Brian was the pilot. She'd always been proud of him and the job he did. There'd been fear, too, of course, but when you married a Marine, that was just part of the package.

She lifted one hand to shield her eyes as she followed the jet's progress across the sky.

"Pretty sight," a voice from behind her said, loud enough to be heard over the music still pouring from the house into the hot, summer air.

Tina sucked in a breath and slowly turned around to look up at him. She hadn't heard him drive up. Hadn't expected him to come back home in the middle of the day. In fact, she'd figured him for spending as much time away from the house as possible.

Yet, here he was.

Taller than most pilots, Brian used to complain about the cockpit of an F-18 being a tight fit. But she'd always liked the fact that he was so much taller than her. Unless she was on the ground having to tip her head all the way back just to meet his eyes. She stood up, brushing grass off her knees and then peeling the worn, stained, gardening gloves from her hands.

The sun shone directly into her eyes, silhouetting Brian, throwing his face into shadow. But she felt him watching her and knew that his gaze was locked on her. "What'd you say?" she finally asked, then remembered and said, "Oh. The jet. Yes, it is pretty."

"Didn't mean the jet, but, yeah," he said, "it looked good, too."

Tina felt a rush of warmth spin through her and told herself that a compliment from Brian meant nothing. Only that he was alive and breathing. He'd always been smooth. Always known just what to say. Known how to talk her down from a mad and how to talk her *out* of her panties.

Instantly, memories dazzled her body and the resulting warmth turned to heat and Tina had to fight to keep her knees from wobbling.

"Brian—"

"Tina—"

They started talking together, then each of them stopped and laughed shortly, uncomfortably. A twist of regret tightened in her chest as she acknowledged that discomfort. How had they come to this? she wondered. How had the passion, the love they'd once felt for each other dissolved into this awkward courtesy between strangers?

"You go first," he said tightly.

Shaking her head, she said, "No, it's okay. You go ahead."

Nodding, he jammed his hands into the front pockets of his jeans, rocked on his heels and shifted his gaze to one side briefly before slamming back into hers. "Tina, this isn't easy for me, but…"

While he talked, Tina watched him. And as she watched, her brain, dazzled at first by his unexpected arrival, began to kick in. She noticed the way he held his head. The shrug of his shoulders. The way he stood and the way one corner of his mouth tilted up when he spoke. But it wasn't just how he looked that was different. It was how he *felt*. Or rather, how he *wasn't* making *her* feel. There was no buzz of electricity jumping up and down her spine. There was no hum of energy bristling between them. And no matter what else had passed between them, they'd always shared a combustible chemistry.

Whenever she was near Brian, the very air changed, and she felt that tingle right down to her toes.

Except, at the moment, she felt absolutely *nothing*.

As her brain calculated all of this information and more, Tina's temper flared.

"…I know I don't have the right to ask you to do anything," he was saying.

She should call him on it now. He deserved it. Had to be Connor, she told herself. Aidan wouldn't have tried it. In seconds, dozens of thoughts raced through her mind as she tried to decide how to handle the last of the Reilly triplets. When the solution finally dawned on her, she smiled.

So did he. "See? I knew you'd be reasonable. No sense in you staying here when it would just make it awkward for both of us."

"Awkward?" she said on a deep, throaty purr. "Brian, honey, we know each other way too well to be awkward together."

"Huh?" He looked confused.

Good. Tina chuckled gleefully inside, but on the outside, she gave him a sultry smile and stepped close enough to walk her fingers up his chest and then stroke his cheek. "I missed you, Brian," she breathed and took a deep breath before letting it out slowly. "I'm...*lonely*."

She let that one word hover in the air between them and watched with some small sense of satisfaction as panic lit up Connor's eyes just before he backed up a step. "Now, Tina, I don't think you really mean that and—"

"Brian, baby," she cooed, closing in on him with unerring instinct, "haven't you missed me, too?"

"Uh, sure." He looked around wildly for help that wasn't coming.

Tina moved in even closer and reaching up, wrapped her arms around his neck and leaned into him, pressing her breasts to his chest. He pulled his hands free of his pockets and tried to hold her away from him. But she'd felt the frantic beat of his heart and knew she'd gotten payback. "So, kiss me, Connor."

"Kiss you—" he broke off and looked down into her eyes. *"Connor?"*

"You idiot." She released him and took a step back while having the pleasure of watching him mentally trying to backtrack.

"Look, Tina…"

"Did you really think you could fool me?" she demanded hotly, all kidding aside.

"Whoa," he said, swallowing hard and shaking his head. "Tina, I don't know what you're talking about—"

The temper she'd felt building a moment before leaped into pure rage, and she wouldn't have been surprised to feel steam coming out of her ears. "Sure you do. But it looks like both you *and* Brian have forgotten a few things. See, I can tell you guys apart. Always could. Remember?"

He scraped one hand across his jaw, then shoved both hands into his pockets again. "Okay, it was a bad idea."

"Bad idea?" She stared up at him in openmouthed fascination. "I don't believe you guys. What? Are we in junior high? What were you supposed to do, Connor? Talk me into leaving so Brian wouldn't have to face me again?"

A short bark of laughter shot from his throat as he pulled his hands free of his pockets and held them up in surrender. "Come on, Tina. It was just—"

"What?" she demanded, moving in on him, keeping pace as he backed up toward his—*Brian's*—car parked in the driveway. "A joke?"

"No!" He scraped one hand across his jaw and stumbled over the hose that had been stretched out across the lawn. He recovered quickly, did a fast two-step and kept moving toward the safety of the car. "Brian just thought—I mean *I* just thought—"

Muffin and Peaches sent up a din of barks and frantic yelps that had Connor throwing an uneasy glance at the screen door.

"This was his idea, wasn't it?" she challenged, so disgusted with Brian *and* Connor, she could barely squeeze the words out of her tight throat.

"No—yeah—I mean…" He looked at her again and threw both hands high in an *I'm innocent* pose that didn't convince her. "It was just an idea."

"A bad one."

"I see that now." He nodded and swallowed hard. "Believe me. But hey, you gave me a couple bad minutes there, too, you know."

"Where's Brian?" she demanded, still moving closer.

"Now, Tina…"

She glared at him as she saw his mind working

fast, trying to come up with a stall. Then she realized that the triplets solidarity would work against her here. Connor wouldn't squeal on his brother. But then, he didn't have to.

"Never mind," she said tightly. "He has to come back here sometime, doesn't he?"

"Uh, you bet." At last, he backed into the car and reaching behind him, grabbed the door latch. Unwilling to take his gaze off her, he opened the door and slid inside as fast as he was able.

But before he could slam the car door shut, Tina grabbed the edge of it and leaned in toward him. It did her heart good to watch those blue eyes so much like Brian's suddenly sparkle with trepidation.

Served him right.

"Now you listen to me, Connor Reilly…"

"Oh, I'm listening, Tina."

"You tell your brother that I want to talk to him."

"Right." He reached for the keys dangling from the ignition and fired up the engine. "I'll tell him."

"And don't you even think of trying this on me again, Connor."

He looked at her for a long moment, then slowly gave her a wide smile. "Not a chance, ma'am. You're just too scary."

Now that the first, furious blast of anger had dissipated a little, she could appreciate the humor in the situation. At least as far as Connor was concerned.

Tina's mouth twitched, but she refused to smile back at him.

"You know something, Tina?" he said softly, "even though you just took about five years off my life, it's good to have you home."

Now she did smile. It would have been impossible not to. No woman could stand against a Reilly man for very long. "Go away, Connor."

"Yes, ma'am."

She stepped back, slammed the car door, then stood and watched as he pulled out and drove away. The minute he'd turned the corner though, Tina headed for the house. If she and Brian were going to have a confrontation, then she'd be damned if she'd do it sweaty and dirty from the garden.

Four

Connor's laughter still ringing in his ears, Brian winced as he pulled into the driveway. What his brother had found so damned funny, Tina was sure to be pissed about.

He'd known going in that the trick would never work. Just the fact that he'd let Connor try to put one over on Tina proved the level of Brian's desperation. And in a weird sort of way, he was glad it hadn't. At least he knew that Tina could still tell him apart from his brothers. It had always been like that. Even though everyone else considered the Reilly triplets interchangeable, Tina was different. So different from every other woman on the face of the damn planet, that if Brian couldn't get her to leave town soon, he was a dead man. He'd never survive the bet with his brothers.

Hell, any other time, Tina's visit would have been bad enough. She was a distraction no matter how you looked at it. But now, when he was already a man on the edge, Tina was enough to push him over.

He'd never wanted another woman as badly as Tina. And that still held true. They'd been apart for five years, but just knowing she was in town had his body tightening and his blood pumping. Knowing that she was alone, in the house next door, made sleep impossible and every waking moment a torture.

Oh, yeah. He was in bad shape.

Still grumbling about the coming confrontation with Tina, he stepped out of the car into the cool of twilight. The sun was down, the first stars were just starting to wink into life and jasmine scented the air.

The front door to the main house was open, lamplight spilling into the darkening yard, laying out a path of welcome that he was willing to bet Tina hadn't meant for him. Brian scowled at the house and told himself he didn't give a damn what she thought about his plan. He'd had to try, and it didn't really matter if she was mad about it or not. He didn't owe her anything anymore. They were exes.

So why then, did he feel so blasted guilty?

And so damned hesitant about facing her?

Hell, he was a Marine.

Trained for combat.

Which, he told himself as he started for the door, might just come in handy when talking to Tina Coretti Reilly.

He took the steps in a couple of long strides and stood in the slice of lamplight, staring through the screen door. From the living room, came the muted, plaintive wail of good jazz playing on the stereo. The dogs had to be outside, or they'd have had their nasty little faces pressed to the screen in an attempt to chew right through the mesh and get to him. So, there was one good point. No dogs to deal with.

He knocked. No response.

He knocked again, louder this time.

"Brian?" she called, "Is that you?"

"Yeah, it's me."

"Come in."

Well, so far, she sounded reasonable. Good. That was good. He stepped into the house, walked through the living room and tossed his USMC cap at the closest table. He rounded the corner into the kitchen and found her sitting at the table, a glass of white wine in her hand.

She was mad. He could see it. Her eyes danced

with it. And damned if she didn't look great. That extra sparkle in her eyes appealed to him, which let Brian know he was in deep trouble.

"Sit down."

"No, thanks," he said, letting his gaze slide over her smooth, tanned legs, her pale green cotton shorts and one of the skimpiest tank tops he'd ever seen. No, he wouldn't sit down. He wouldn't be staying that long. Couldn't afford to be around a woman who could torment him this easily. So, best to just say what he had to say and get out of there. "Look, Tina, I'm sorry about—"

"—sending Connor to get rid of me?" she finished for him, then paused for a sip of wine.

He lifted one shoulder in a shrug. "Well, yeah."

"That's it?" She swiveled on her chair, crossed her legs and swung her foot lazily.

Her toes were painted a soft pink and she wore a silver toe ring. *Oh, man.*

"That's all you've got to say?" One finely arched dark eyebrow lifted.

Brian scraped one hand across his jaw. "What do you want from me? I gave it a shot." Oh, he had to get out of the room. Fast.

She stood up, set her wine on the table and took a step toward him. Her tank top had those tiny little spaghetti straps and they were the *only* straps across her smooth shoulders. No bra. His gaze dipped to her pebbled nipples, outlined to perfection beneath the clingy, white fabric. *Oh, man.*

"Why are you so anxious to get me out of town, Brian?"

"Not anxious," he said, then corrected silently, *desperate.* But he couldn't say that to her. Couldn't let her know what she could still do to him with a single look.

"Connor didn't fool me," she said, hitching one hip a little higher than the other and tapping her bare toes against the cream-colored linoleum.

"Yeah, I know," Brian said, doing his best to keep his gaze locked with hers. It wasn't safe, God knew, since her big brown eyes had a way of sucking him in and holding him close. But it was safer than admiring her skin or the way her tank top rode up on her flat belly or the way her shorts molded so nicely to the curve of her behind. Oh, yeah. Safer.

"Why'd you do it, Brian?" she asked, and her amazing eyes locked on to him again.

She was like a damn polygraph. Looking into Tina's eyes *forced* a man to tell the truth. At least, that's how her deep brown eyes had always affected him.

"Because," he muttered thickly, "I just don't want you around."

Her head snapped back as if he'd slapped her, and he cursed himself silently. Then she took a step closer and Brian caught of a whiff of her cologne. She still wore the stuff she'd worn five years ago. A magical blend of flowers and citrus, it smelled like summer and warm nights in her arms and, damn it, he told himself, *stop breathing*.

A heartbeat later, she'd recovered. "That's honest, at least. Why?"

He tore his gaze from her eyes, stepped past her and picked up her wine. Chugging a long drink of the cold, white liquid, he swallowed hard and glanced over his shoulder at her. "What's the point, Tina?"

Tina watched him avoid looking directly at her and a ping of something sad and empty resounded inside her. She'd been so furious all afternoon, waiting to face him, and now that the time was here, all she could think was how different they were together now. The attraction was still there, no doubt about that.

She'd seen his eyes glaze over when he first walked into the room and she'd felt that instant rush of something powerful sweep through her. But then he'd distanced himself without moving a step and she'd felt as though she could reach for him for years and never really touch him.

But she wouldn't let herself be hurt. Wouldn't allow him to chase her off. Not until she'd done what she came here to do. And if that meant that she had to fight past his defenses, then she was just the woman to do it.

"Geez, Brian," she said, just a little hotly, "does

there have to be a point? Can't we just be friends again?"

He laughed shortly and set her wineglass carefully back down. "We were never friends, Tina."

True. She hated to admit that even to herself, but it was true. From the moment they'd first met, they'd been lovers. There'd been no "friendship" period between them. It was all flash fires and fireworks. It was need and hunger and passion.

If they'd been friends, too, maybe they would have lasted. Maybe Brian wouldn't have been able to walk away as easily as he had.

"We could be now," she said.

"Why?"

"Because you meant something to me once," she said and hoped to heaven he couldn't see that he *still* meant something. What, she wasn't sure, but it was there. "Because what we had was good."

"What we had is over."

His quiet voice jabbed at her with the strength of a punch to the stomach, but she didn't waver. Didn't let him see how much it hurt to know that all he wanted from her was for her to be gone.

Instead, she asked the question that had been haunting her for five years. After all, if he wanted to be distant, he could give her the reason. He could tell her why he'd suddenly announced he wanted a divorce—without ever saying why.

"It's over because *you* decided it would be."

He sighed. "Tina—"

"Tell me why, Brian," she said and took a step closer. She saw his blue eyes darken, his expression tighten. "Tell me why you threw us away and maybe I'll think about leaving."

She wouldn't but he didn't have to know that.

"It was five years ago, Tina. Let it go."

"You still won't tell me?" she asked. "Not even for the chance of getting rid of me?"

One corner of his mouth quirked, and Tina felt a tug of reaction down low in her belly. Brian Reilly had one great mouth. Instantly, her brain filled with images of just what that mouth was capable of. Memories crowded into her brain, stealing her breath and making her blood hum with a sense of expectation.

"You wouldn't leave," he said, shaking his head. "Not until you're good and ready."

Still feeling the rush of attraction, she smiled and admitted, "True."

"You always were a hard head."

"Coming from the Rock of Gibraltar, not much of an insult."

"Didn't mean it as an insult," he admitted. "I always sort of enjoyed our arguments—at least, I enjoyed the making up part."

A rush of heat swamped her, and Tina had to

breathe deeply a few times, just to keep her brain on track. "If you enjoyed our marriage so damn much, why'd you—"

"So, why're *you* here?" He interrupted her neatly, clearly refusing to talk about the past. Again. Shifting position slightly, he leaned one hip against the chipped, blue tile counter. "Why now?"

He looked dangerous.

Always had, which she had to admit, if only silently, had been part of his appeal. Black hair, blue eyes, a broad chest, narrow hips and the ability to wear blue jeans like no one else she'd ever known. Of course he could get to her in a heartbeat. There probably wasn't a woman on the planet between the ages of sixteen and sixty he wouldn't affect.

Swallowing hard against a sudden knot of need that had lodged in her throat, Tina said, "Nana went to Italy. She needed help with Muffin and Peaches."

"And that's it?" he asked, eyeing her suspiciously. "The only reason? You didn't talk to my brothers or anything?"

"What are you talking about?" she asked, trying and failing to read his expression. "The only one of your brothers I've talked to is Connor."

He didn't look as though he completely believed her, and she wondered what he was thinking. Wondered just what else was going on. And even as she wondered, Tina knew she'd never find out from Brian, so she'd just have to snoop around a little.

Brian had the decency to wince when she said Connor's name. "Yeah. Sorry about that. I knew it wouldn't work and still let him try." Clearing his throat, he added wryly, "If it's any consolation, you scared the hell out of him."

Tina smiled. "Actually, yes, it is some consolation. But it doesn't tell me what I want to know. Which is, why'd you do it in the first place? Why is it so important to get me out of town?"

His features closed up and a shutter dropped over his eyes. It was the only way to describe the sudden distance in him. One moment he'd been less than a foot away from her and the next, he might as well have been on Venus.

"Doesn't matter anymore."

"It does to me," she admitted.

"Just forget it all right?" He pushed away from the counter and half turned toward the back door.

"The dogs are out there."

"Damn it." He did a quick about-face and stalked across the kitchen and into the living room.

Tina was right behind him.

He snatched up his cap off the table and marched across the dimly lit living room to the front door. As he stepped out, Tina reached for him and grabbed his upper arm.

He stopped dead, as if he'd been shot. He looked down at her hand on his arm, then slowly lifted his gaze to hers.

She knew what he wanted, but she didn't let go of him. It wasn't only stubbornness that had her hanging on, it was also the direct heat that had zipped through her body at the first touch of him. Electric. It felt as though live wires were dancing and skittering inside her veins and she didn't want to lose that sensation so quickly. It had been way too long since she'd felt it.

"I'm not leaving," she said firmly, meeting his gaze so tightly, she saw the shift of emotions in his eyes, but they came and went too fast to identify them. "I'm going to be here for three weeks, Brian. So you'd better find a way to deal with that."

His jaw clenched and she was pretty sure he was grinding his teeth. Which, actually, made her feel a lot better about the whole situation. Sure he wanted her out of town. Sure, he didn't want her to touch him.

Because whether he wanted to admit it or not, he experienced the same short-circuiting sense of excitement from her that she did from him.

Which meant, all in all, that Tina was going to have an easier time seducing him than she'd thought she would.

After all, that's why she was here, right?

To get Brian into bed.

To get pregnant.

And then to leave.

She let him go on that thought because the idea of leaving was less pleasant than the other thoughts had been and she didn't want him to see any hesitation on her face.

"Fine." He nodded and stepped out onto the porch. Settling his cap on his head, he looked at her from eyes shadowed by the black brim of the cap. "Three weeks. I can handle it if you can."

Then he stomped down the steps, circled the house and headed for the stairs to his apartment. The dogs erupted into howls, yips and barks and Tina chuckled when she heard Brian mutter, "Shut up, you little beasts."

Handle it?

He might think he'd be able to handle it, but Tina knew that she was getting to him. Knew that before the next week was up, she'd have him just where she wanted him.

The only question was, would *she* be able to handle leaving him again when the three weeks were over?

Bright and early the next morning, Tina dressed carefully in cream-colored linen slacks and a pale russet blouse. Then she snapped Peaches and Muffin onto their leashes and headed down the street.

It felt strange to go for a walk. Too long in California, she thought. Out there, people drove a half a block to a store rather than walking. Traffic was awful because carpooling had never taken off. Californians liked their cars and their sense of independence too much to share rides. They wanted to be able to go, when and where they wanted to.

Here in Baywater though, the quiet streets were made for walking. The sidewalks rose and fell like waves on the ocean as they climbed over tree roots. But when the sidewalks split, the city came out and patched the cement. A much better solution to Tina's way of thinking, than the California answer to growing trees—which was to rip them out at the roots and plant newer, smaller trees. And then when they grew, rip *them* out and start over again.

The trees in Baywater, left alone to do what trees did best, stretched out leafy arms toward each other, making thick green arches over the wide streets. Kids rolled by on skateboards, neighbors worked in the garden and everyone had a swing on the front porch, just made for sitting and watching the world roll by.

God, she'd missed it.

"Hi, Mrs. Donovan," she called and grinned when the old woman pruning her roses lifted a hand and smiled.

"That's another thing," Tina said, talking to the dogs as they pulled her forward, "neighbors actually talk to you here. They smile. Nobody ever smiles on the freeway."

The dogs didn't care.

Tina'd never really thought about the differences between South Carolina and California much before. Mainly, she guessed now, because if she had, the homesickness would have crippled her. Always before, her visits to her grandmother were quick and so full of activity or just plain sitting at the kitchen table talking, that she didn't get the chance to wander around her hometown. To appreciate the quiet beauty and the peaceful atmosphere. To give herself a chance to wind down from all the hurry up and wait in California.

Now that she had, it was addictive.

Muffin and Peaches strained at their leashes, wandering back and forth until the twin, red leather straps were hopelessly tangled and they were just short of strangling each other in their enthusiasm. Tina laughed and skipped over Peaches as she darted backward to smell something she'd missed.

Quickly, Tina bent down and did a hand over hand thing with the leashes until they were straight again. "Now, how about single file?" she muttered and laughed as Muffin's tongue did a quick swipe across her chin.

Straightening up, she started walking again and as the dogs' tiny nails clicked against the sidewalk, she thought about her latest plan.

Tina had spent a long, sleepless night thinking about Brian and what he'd said. Or more importantly, what he hadn't said. And just before the first streaks of light crossed the dawn sky, she'd realized what she had to do.

Talk to the one Reilly brother who wouldn't lie to her. The one man she knew who was obliged, by virtue of his career, to tell her the absolute truth.

Father Liam.

Five

The rectory at St. Sebastian's Catholic church was old and elegant. Built in the same style as the small church, the rectory, or priest's house, looked like a tiny castle, squatting alongside the church itself. Ancient magnolia trees filled the yard and their wide, silky leaves rustled in a barely felt breeze as Tina approached.

The rectory's weathered gray brick seemed to absorb the summer sunlight, holding it close and giving the building a sense of warmth, welcome. Sunshine glinted off the leaded windows and the petunias crowding huge terra cotta pots on the porch were splotches of bright purple, red and white in the shadows.

Muffin and Peaches raced up the sidewalk, dragging Tina in their wake and she was laughing as she rang the doorbell. An older woman, tall, with graying red hair and sharp green eyes, opened the door and asked, "May I help you?"

"Hello. I'd like to see Father Liam, if he's here."

The woman gave Tina a quick but thorough up and down look, then nodded and stepped back, issuing a silent invitation. Tina stepped into the room and gathered up the leashes tightly, keeping the dogs close at hand. She looked around and smiled at the dark wood paneling, the faded colors in the braided rugs and the sunlight spilling through windows to form tiny, diamond shapes on the gleaming wood floor.

"He's right in there," the woman said, reaching for the leashes. She spared a sniff as she added, "I'll take your dogs to the backyard while you talk to Father."

Before Tina could agree or not, the woman had Muffin and Peaches in hand and headed down a long, narrow hallway toward the back of the house. Shrugging, Tina crossed the hall to the door indicated, knocked and pushed it open.

Liam was sitting in an overstuffed chair, his feet up on a magazine-littered coffee table. He dropped the book he was reading, grinned and jumped to his feet when he saw her. "Tina!"

He crossed the room in a few long strides and enveloped her in a fierce, tight hug. Tina held on for a long minute, grateful for the warm welcome. Brian had certainly made it a point to let her know she wasn't wanted. Getting this kind of reaction from Liam soothed her bruised feelings.

When he grabbed her shoulders and held her back for a long look, he grinned. "You look terrific. And it's so good to see you."

"Thanks, Liam. Good to see you, too."

"Come in, sit down."

"Sure you're not busy?" She glanced around, but all she saw were the magazines and the open book, now lying on the carpet.

"Nope. Just reading a murder mystery, but it can wait." He took a seat beside her on the couch. "When did you get in? How long are you here for?"

"A few days ago and three weeks," she said, smiling. Priest or not, Liam Reilly was the kind of man women noticed. His black hair, longer than his brothers' military cuts, was thick and wavy and his deep blue eyes were framed by long, black lashes. Tall and lean, he walked with an easy grace and his mouth was usually curved in a grin designed to win female hearts. There'd been a lot of disappointed women in Baywater when Liam entered the priesthood.

He looked at her carefully, tipped his head to one side and asked, "What's wrong?"

She laughed shortly. "You must be psychic as well as a priest."

"Nope," he assured her with a grin. "Just incredibly handsome and charming." Then he added, "But I know my people and my instincts are telling me there's something bothering you."

"Score one for Father Liam."

"Good. Now why don't you tell me what it is."

Where to start? It had seemed like a good idea at the time, coming here, to talk to Liam. But priest or not, he was also Brian's brother. Would he really side with Tina against his family? Or would he just clam up and keep whatever secrets Brian was hiding?

"You're thinking," Liam said softly. "I can practically see the wheels turning behind your eyes."

"I'm just wondering if maybe I shouldn't have come."

"Of course you should come to see me." He reached out and took one of her hands with both of his. "Especially if there's something bothering you."

A knock at the door sounded and the older woman poked her head into the room. "Would your guest like some tea, Father?"

Covertly, Liam shook his head at Tina, but she ignored him. It had been a long walk. "That would be great, thank you."

When the woman was gone again, Liam sighed. "Mrs. Hannigan makes the world's worst tea, poor woman."

"Sorry."

"Doesn't matter," he said on a sigh. "I'm almost used to it now anyway. But it may kill you."

"I'm tough," Tina assured him.

"Not tough enough to hide whatever's bothering you. So spill it."

She did. Right or wrong, she'd made the choice to come to Liam, so she would see it through. She started at the beginning and hit only the high points. How she'd decided to become a mother and how the only man she wanted to father her child was Brian and how she was now starting to worry about it all because Brian was so determined to stay away from her and "…so," she said, winding the story up, "Brian had Connor try to get rid of me, and then refused to tell me why he wants me out of town so badly. I know something's up, I just don't know *what*."

Liam laughed.

Throughout her story, he'd watched her eyes and she'd noticed first, understanding, and then the amused sparkle in his concerned blue gaze. But outright laughter seemed a little harsh.

"Hello?" she said, reaching out to slug his upper arm. "I came here for comfort, you know. And some answers."

"I know, I know," Liam said, still laughing as he rubbed his arm and then stood up to greet Mrs. Hannigan as she reentered the study. He took the tray from her and set it down on the coffee table. Once the woman was gone again, Liam poured a murky brown liquid into one of the tall glasses filled with ice. Giving it a wary look, he passed it to Tina. "Drink that, if you're feeling brave, and I'll explain."

She did and at the first sip, she shuddered and felt a caffeine reaction punch through her like a bunched fist. The woman must have brewed the tea for days. It was almost thick enough to chew.

"I did warn you," Liam said, obviously watching her reaction.

"Right." She set the glass onto the tray, then turned to face her ex-brother-in-law again. "Start talking, Liam."

He did. And when he was finished, she just stared at him for a long minute.

"You bet your brothers that they couldn't abstain from sex for three months."

"Yep." He grinned again and leaned back into the faded floral couch.

"You're a *priest*."

He held up one finger. "I'm also a Reilly. And I know my brothers. They'll never make it."

"And you're enjoying this."

"Oh, yeah," he said with relish and rubbed his palms together. *"And,"* he said, "with you back in town, the odds just went even higher in my favor."

"How do you figure?"

Liam smirked at her. "Please. You and Brian are *meant* to be together."

"We're divorced, remember?" Tina cringed inwardly at the word. She still didn't like it. Still hadn't accepted it, even five years after the event.

She'd dated over the past five years, but Brian had always been there. In her heart. In her mind. He was the shadow she couldn't quite lose. The memory she couldn't quite forget. He was the love of her life. Or, at least, he had been.

Liam waved one hand at her, waving away her objections. "I blessed your marriage," he said. "And the marriages I bless don't dissolve."

"Nice in theory," she said.

He shook his head, sat up and leaned in toward her. "Tina, you guys are both Catholic. You know as well as I do that Catholic marriages are forever."

"Until the state of South Carolina says they're not," she reminded him.

"*My* boss has a lot more clout than the governor," he said, with a smile.

"I guess so," she admitted, but shook her head again.

"Look," Liam told her, giving one of her hands a squeeze. "Brian's a man on the edge already. It wouldn't take much for you to push him over."

"So my priest is suggesting I seduce a man who isn't my husband?"

He winked at her. "According to the church,

you're still married. Besides, this is a poor parish. We need that new roof."

In spite of everything, Tina laughed. "You Reillys are really something."

"We thank you."

"I don't think Brian will," she mused, reaching for her iced tea, before remembering and drawing her hand back empty.

Liam scooted around on the couch, dropped one arm across Tina's shoulders and gave her a brief hug. "That's where you're wrong, Tina. Brian made a big mistake letting you go. Maybe it's time you showed him how big a mistake it was."

She leaned into the solid comfort of Liam's embrace and thought about everything he'd said. As she did, she smiled. The only reason Brian would be trying so hard to get rid of her, is if he didn't trust himself around her. Which told Tina that seducing Brian Reilly just got a lot easier.

Now all she had to do, was convince herself that she really was doing the right thing.

No problem.

By the time Brian got home from the base, he was worn out. He'd done everything he could to run himself ragged so that he'd sleep tonight, without the taunting dreams he'd been experiencing the past few nights.

Ever since Tina came back to town, he'd hardly dared close his eyes. The minute he did, she was there. Surrounding him in living breathing color. He could feel her, hear her, smell her. She filled his mind and tortured him in his sleep.

For three nights running, he'd awakened in the middle of the night, with his only recourse an ice-cold shower.

Not the way he wanted to spend the next two and a half weeks.

So until she left, he'd just work himself into the ground so exhaustion would take care of shutting down his too-busy mind. Today, after taking his jet up for some qualifying runs, he'd hit the weight room, then talked three of the guys into doing a five-mile run. The summer heat had pounded at them and the humidity was enough to make a grown man weep.

But as he pulled into the driveway that night, even exhaustion couldn't completely stamp out the instantaneous reaction his body went into at Tina's nearness.

The house was lit up like a fistful of birthday candles. Every light in the living room was on and a wide slice of lamplight spilled from the kitchen windows onto the flower-lined driveway. Music, something soft and entreating, drifted through the partially opened window overlooking the drive. It all looked warm and friendly, but he knew that inside that house was the biggest danger of all.

Brian walked along the driveway and stopped just short of stepping into the patch of light. Instead, he stayed in the shadows and looked through the kitchen window. Tina was there, alone, dancing slowly to the beat of the music playing on the stereo. His breath caught as he watched her move around the room in time to the music. Her body, long and lean and tanned, looked great in the shorts and skimpy tank top she wore. Her hips swayed, her eyes closed and when she lifted her arms like a gypsy dancer, it was all he could do to keep from storming into the room and grabbing her.

He rubbed both hands across his face and told himself to get a grip. But it was impossible. When he was thirty thousand feet above the ground, in the cockpit of his F-18, blasting across the sky, he felt in control. Sure of himself. But with his feet firmly on the ground and Tina in Baywater, Brian was a drowning man going down for the third time.

God, why was this so hard?

He'd let her go five years ago because he'd believed, deep in his heart, he was doing the right thing for her. For both of them. And it was fairly easy to keep himself convinced of that when she was on the opposite end of the country.

But now that she was home again.

Here.

Within arm's reach—he wasn't so sure anymore.

As that thought skittered uneasily through his mind, he headed toward the stairs, determined to ignore Tina and sneak—correction—*go* home without seeing her. And take another cold shower.

Of course, he'd forgotten about the damn dogs.

Muffin and Peaches erupted into a cacophony of sound that damn near deafened him and Brian shot the closed, backyard gate a furious glare. The little mutts had it in for him.

Suddenly the back door flew open, he turned to look and there was Tina, silhouetted in the doorway. His heart did a quick spin, jump and lurch and it was a second or two before he could draw an easy breath.

"Quiet, girls," she said and instantly, silence dropped over them.

It was almost eerie.

"Thanks," Brian said with another glare for the two little meatheads hidden from sight behind the gate. "I'm still not sure why they hate me."

Tina cocked a hip and leaned one shoulder against the doorjamb. "Maybe they love you and they're just too shy to show it."

He snorted. "Yeah, that's it." He lifted a hand and started for the stairs.

"Brian?"

He stopped and looked back, wishing he could just keep walking. "Yeah?"

"Would you mind taking a look at Nana's TV?"

"What?"

"The TV. It's all fuzzed out and I can't get a picture."

Go into the house? With her? Alone? Feeling like he did right now?

Not a good idea.

She saw him hesitate and spoke up before he could say no. "You're not afraid of me, are you?"

Brian snapped her a glance. He knew exactly what she was doing. She was challenging him. Throwing down a gauntlet. Making a dare. Because she knew he'd respond to it, damn it.

"Don't be ridiculous," he said tightly.

"Good. Then come around the front and you won't have to fight your way past the dogs."

She let him in the front door and the music from the stereo reached out for him. Tina stood back for him to come inside, but he took a whiff of her perfume as he passed, just to make sure the torture continued. Seriously, he should try to find a way not to breathe when she was around. Because the only way he'd be safe from Tina was when he was buried six feet under and even then, he had a feeling she'd still be able to get a reaction out of him.

"What's wrong with the TV?" he asked, moving directly for it, hoping to make the repair and get out of there as fast as possible.

"Now, if I knew that, I'd have fixed it, right?"

She stood right beside him and from the corner of

his eye, he got way too good a picture of her smooth, silky-looking legs. He shifted his gaze to the TV, telling himself to do the job and move on.

Moving closer, Tina squatted down beside him until they were practically nose to nose. Her brown eyes glittered in the lamplight and her perfume reached for him, invading him. "You're in my light," he muttered.

"Sorry," she said, but didn't move.

Muttering beneath his breath, Brian punched the power button on the TV and was rewarded instantly with a screen full of flickering gray snow. No picture. No sound. Great.

"What do you think?" she asked.

"I don't know," he said, turning to look at her and finding her mouth was just a breath away from his. Why the hell was she leaning into him like that? How did she expect him to fix a damn television when she was practically sitting on his lap?

His body tightened, his breath shortened and his heartbeat took off at a wild gallop. Gritting his teeth, Brian said, "You need to move so I can look behind the set."

"Okay." She shrugged and the skinny little strap of her pale blue tank top slid down her right shoulder.

Brian swallowed hard.

"What's the matter?" she asked, brown eyes wide with innocence.

"Nothing," he said, and inched past her to see the back of the television. He pried off the black plastic casing and stared blindly at the wires and chips he'd exposed. If his brain was working, he could probably figure this out, but at the moment, the only thing working was his groin.

"Wow," she murmured, leaning in to get a look at the television's inner workings, "I wouldn't even know where to start."

Her hair was in his face now and the soft, silkiness of it brushed against his skin and filled his mind with the scent of flowers. Brian closed his eyes tightly, grabbed her by the shoulders and pushed her out of the way as quickly as he could. And even then, it didn't diminish the flash of heat rippling from his fingers, straight up his arms to rattle around in his chest. Touching Tina was like touching a live electrical wire.

"If you'll stay the hell outta the way," he muttered, not daring a look at her again, "I'll try to fix it."

"Pardon me," she said, but she smiled and didn't move away. Instead, she settled down and crossed her legs. Leaning her elbows on her knees, she rested her chin on her hands and watched him. "You always could fix just about anything," she said.

He tried to shrug that away. He wasn't going to be led down memory lane. Not when he was already on pretty shaky ground. "I was always good with my hands."

"Yeah," Tina said on a soft sigh, "I remember."

Oh man, he was in deep trouble here and sinking fast.

"Look," he said as he backed out from behind the TV while still trying to keep a safe distance from her, "maybe you'd better call a TV guy tomorrow and—"

"What?"

He looked back over his shoulder at her and narrowed his eyes suspiciously. Then he held up a thick black cable with a silver connection head on it. "I think I found the problem," he said.

"Really?" Her lips twitched and the dark brown of her eyes shone with amusement and…something else.

Tearing his gaze from hers, Brian turned around, screwed the silver head back into the wall plate and instantly the picture and sound on the television set blasted into life.

Tina reached out and shut it off.

"Why'd you unplug the cable, Tina?"

She shrugged again and this time, the strap on her other shoulder slid down. The only thing holding her tank top up now, was the swell of her breasts.

"Why've you been avoiding me, Brian?"

"Doing things my way now?" he asked, "Answering questions with a question?"

"Oh," she said and shifted around until she was kneeling on the floor right in front of him. "I have an answer, I just don't think you'll like it."

"Try me."

"Okay," she said smiling, "but remember, you asked for it.

Then she leaned forward, took his face between her palms and kissed him until Brian was sure his eyeballs were going to pop right out of his head.

And he wouldn't have missed them.

Six

Instantly, Tina realized her mistake.

She'd thought it a simple thing, getting Brian to kiss her. After all, years ago, she'd had plenty of practice in turning Brian on.

But what she hadn't counted on, was her *own* reaction to the kiss.

She'd planned on being the logical one.

The cool-headed one.

The one in charge.

But there was no one in charge now.

They were on a runaway train and with every passing second, that train picked up speed.

Brian pulled her close and with one hand at the

back of her head, held her in a bruising grip. Her heart raced, her blood pumped and her brain clicked off.

All that was left was sensation.

The feel of Brian's mouth on hers. The warm slide of his tongue as he tasted her, explored her. The strength of his hands on her body and the hot brush of his breath on her cheek.

He groaned tightly and Tina felt an identical response shuddering within her. It had been too long since she'd felt anything like this. Too long since her blood sparkled like freshly opened champagne. Too long since her brain fuzzed over and her body tingled.

She kissed him back, putting everything she had into it, claiming his mouth with the same ferocity he took hers. Their tongues tangled together in a wild dance of need and she held on to him as the earth beneath her seemed to tilt dangerously.

His hands moved over her, roughly, demanding, and she loved it. His calloused palms scraped her flesh and sent chills racing along her spine. He tore his mouth from hers and hungrily trailed his mouth along her neck, following the line of her throat and down, lower and lower until Tina held her breath, let her head fall back and silently prayed for more.

And then he gave her more and she sighed his name like a blessing.

He slid the edge of her tank top down, pushing it

over her breasts until he'd freed them from the fabric and Tina held her breath again, waiting.

"Tina…" he murmured and dipped his head, to take first one, then the other of her nipples into his mouth.

Her breath sighed from her lips as she felt the dazzling sensations rocketing around inside her.

His lips and tongue defined the rigid points and as he suckled at one of her breasts, his fingers teased the other until Tina couldn't think. Couldn't breathe.

He seemed insatiable. As if he couldn't taste enough of her. As if the taste of her were more important than his next breath. And his hands continued to move over her, stroking, sliding, up her back, over her breasts, and down over her hips to her thighs and then inward, to the warmth of her center. He cupped her and even through the linen fabric of the shorts she wore, Tina felt his heat. Felt the incredible pressure of his touch on her and knew she needed more. Needed to feel flesh on flesh.

"Brian," she murmured, kissing his neck, his jaw, nibbling at his bottom lip as he lifted his head to look at her through dazed eyes. "I want you. I want you so much."

Brian struggled for air. It felt as though an iron band was around his chest, squeezing. Every inch of his body was alive and screaming. Need radiated from him, and his instincts were all telling him to stretch her out on the floor and take her, hard and fast.

She rocked her hips against his hand and he groaned, gritting his teeth and fighting the hot flash of desire nearly choking him. He touched her center and even through the soft fabric covering her body, he felt her heat, pulling at him.

"Brian, please—"

He looked at her, meeting her gaze and momentarily, he lost himself in the shadowy depths of her eyes. She wanted him. He wanted her. Why did this have to be any more complicated than that?

But it was.

On too many levels.

Sure, the bet, he thought and knew that one more minute in her arms and he'd throw away the stupid bet and any amount of money for the chance to be with her. But there was more at stake here, too. They'd been apart five years. It hadn't been easy, but it had been the right thing to do. Did he dare risk screwing it all up now, making it harder on both of them, just for the sake of losing himself in her one more time?

Her hips rocked again and she pulled herself closer, tighter, to him. One arm went around her and he allowed himself a moment to revel in the feel of holding her again. To feel her hair soft against his neck, the press of her breasts against his chest and the soft brush of her breath. He knew her sighs, her moans, her every mood.

And he'd missed her more than he'd ever thought possible.

"Brian…"

"Tina," he said her name on a sigh that ripped from his chest and tore free of his soul.

"Don't—" she warned, shaking her head and holding on to him even more tightly. "Don't walk away. Don't deny us—"

He touched her.

Because he wanted to.

Because he *needed* to.

His thumb scraped across the fabric strained tight over her center and Tina reacted instantly. She clutched at his shoulders and opened her legs further, giving him access.

"Touch me, Brian," she whispered and her voice echoed inside his head, his heart.

She turned over onto her back and lay across his lap and Brian shifted his hand far enough to dip beneath the waistband of her shorts, slide across her abdomen and then slide down farther. She rocked in his grasp and her every movement created torture for him as she moved against his hard body, pushing him closer to the ragged edge.

And still he couldn't stop. He could at least have this. Give her this.

His fingers deftly moved beneath her panties to touch her warm, damp flesh.

At his first touch, she arched her back, moving into him, sighing his name. Again and again, he stroked her, at first slowly, teasingly and as she crested closer and closer to her climax, he quickened his rhythm and watched her expressive face as the first tremors of delight shook through her.

Her eyes widened, she bit down hard on her bottom lip and lifted her hips into his hand, his touch, claiming him as much as he claimed her. When she cried out his name, he groaned again and held her while she reached her peak and then fell to earth.

"Brian?" she asked a moment later, lifting both arms to encircle his neck.

She looked more beautiful than he remembered. Her brown eyes were warm and rich and filled now with a lazy satisfaction that was already giving way to new needs. Needs he wouldn't—couldn't—fulfill. Brian grabbed her wrists and shook his head.

"What?" she asked, wariness creeping into her expression.

"I've gotta go," he said and gently lifted her off his lap and pushed himself to his feet. Pain radiated through him and Brian realized he hadn't been that frustrated since he was a kid. A cold shower probably wasn't going to do it this time. With an ache this big, this deep, he'd need an oceanful of cold water.

"Are you kidding?" she demanded, slipping her arms through the straps of her shirt and rearranging her clothing as she stood up to face him. "You're leaving? *Now?*"

"Especially now," he said tightly.

His hands itched to hold her again and other parts of his body were even more interested in getting close again. Deliberately, Brian turned his back on her and stalked to the front door.

"Was that just me, Brian?" she demanded and the tone of her voice prodded him to turn around to meet her gaze just as he hit the front door.

He saw hurt and confusion along with the anger in her eyes and told himself it was his own damn fault. He never should have trusted himself inside this house alone with her.

"Was I alone in there?" she asked, waving one hand behind her toward the living room.

He wanted to say *Yeah, I felt nothing,* because that would surely be the easier way. But the whole Coretti polygraph thing had him in its clutches again and Brian discovered he couldn't lie to her. Not about this.

"No," he said, his voice just a ragged hush of sound, "you weren't alone."

"Then how can you leave?" she asked. "If you feel *anything* of what I'm feeling, how can you leave?"

"Don't you get it, Tina?" he asked, hitting the screen door with the flat of his hand and stepping out onto the porch, "It's *because* I'm feeling what I am that I'm leaving."

She threw her arms across her chest and held on tight. Glaring at him, she snapped, "That makes no sense at all."

His body aching, his mind hurting, his soul emptying, Brian just said, "Yeah, I know."

Then he left.

While he still could.

For the next three days, Brian stayed as far away from Tina as humanly possible. He even considered moving onto the air base for the duration of her visit. But he just couldn't seem to make himself do it. Oh, he didn't trust himself anywhere near her, but at the same time, he didn't want to cheat himself out of at least seeing her from a distance.

Stupid.

Losing control of the situation had been stupid and Brian couldn't even remember *how* he'd lost it. All he could remember was the feel of Tina in his arms again. The soft sigh of her breath. The amazingly responsive woman he'd missed so desperately.

"When are you going to admit it?"

Brian snapped out of his thoughts, which had once again been centered on Tina, and looked at Aidan, across the table from him. "What?"

Aidan sneered at him and jutted his elbow into

Liam's side for emphasis. "D'ya hear that?" he demanded. "He's not even willing to admit to *us* that Tina's getting to him."

"She's not," Brian lied and didn't even feel guilty for it. What was between he and Tina wasn't anyone's business. Not even his brothers.

"Right," Connor said from beside him and reached for a tortilla chip out of the basket in the center of the table. "You're just avoiding going home because you hate the dogs."

"I do," Brian reminded him.

"Uh-huh," Liam put in, "but they've never kept you away from home."

"Fine." He threw both hands up in mock surrender, then reached for his beer. Taking a long swig, he swallowed, then said, "You guys win. Tina's making me nuts. Happy now?"

While his brothers grinned and nodded knowingly, Brian shifted his gaze to the crowd dotting the tables at the Lighthouse. Always, there were families. Kids, of all ages, parents, grandparents. He'd never really paid attention to them before, and maybe that was because it hurt too much to see happy families when his own marriage had ended.

But for some reason, the last few days, all Brian had been noticing were families. His friends and their kids. Military wives driving into Parris Island to hit the Commissary for groceries. And he couldn't help wondering if he and Tina would have had kids by now if he hadn't insisted on a divorce. But following that thought, he wondered if he hadn't saved them both a lot of heartache by ending things when he had.

What if they had had kids, and then divorced? How much harder would everything be? And how unfair to children, torn between two parents.

His gaze fastened on a little girl, no more than two or three. She had dark, curly hair and big brown eyes and looked just as he imagined a daughter of his and Tina's would have looked. She was beautiful, he thought, just a little wistfully. And if a ping of regret sounded in his heart, then he was the only one who would know it.

"I don't know about the rest of you," Aidan said, snagging a chip for himself, "but I'm *real* happy to hear it."

"Oh, me, too," Connor put in. "Good to know I'm not the only one suffering here."

"You guys are lightweights," Liam said with a sly smile.

"Hey," Connor argued, "you've had a few years to deal with this whole, 'no women' thing. We're new to it, thank God."

"And not long for it," Aidan remarked, pointing his beer at Brian. "At least, one of us isn't."

Brian bristled. Sure, things were tougher than he'd

thought and damn, he'd come close to losing the bet—and himself—in Tina the other night. But he'd stayed strong. Stayed dedicated.

Stayed frustrated.

"Don't worry about me, boys," he said tightly. "I'm doing fine."

"Right. That's why you're here with us instead of at home."

Brian ignored Connor and looked at his older brother. "You enjoying this, Liam?"

"I am," he said and cradled his bottle of beer between his palms. Slanting a look at Brian, he said, "You know, maybe there's a *reason* Tina's in town right now."

"Sure. It's fate, huh?" Brian said with a snort.

"Would it be so surprising?"

"Yeah, it would. I don't believe in fate," Brian said flatly. "We make our own decisions."

Aidan and Connor exchanged a glance and a shrug, then kept quiet and listened.

"And if you make the wrong decisions?" Liam asked.

"Then you pay for them."

"Like you're paying now?" Liam mused.

"Who says I'm paying?" Brian argued and when his voice got a little loud, he winced and hunched his shoulders as a woman at the table next to them gave him a quick look. "Damn it, Liam, Tina has nothing to do with this bet."

"I'm not talking about the stupid bet, Brian," his brother said softly, as if only the two of them were at the table. "I'm talking about you letting Tina walk out of your life."

"That's over and done," he murmured, refusing to look at any of his brothers. Instead, he stared at the label on his beer bottle and picked at the edges of it with a thumbnail.

"Is it really?" Liam said on a sigh. "I wonder. If it were really over, wouldn't you feel safe going home?"

Brian snapped him a look then swept his gaze over Connor and Aidan who were both doing their damnedest to look invisible.

Scowling at his sudden discomfort, Brian reached for his wallet, pulled out a bill and tossed it onto the table. Then standing up, he looked down at his brothers, but focused solely on Liam. "I'm trying to stay away from Tina for *her* sake, if you've just really gotta know what I'm doing."

"Okay," Liam said nodding. "I'll buy that, if you can."

"What's that supposed to mean?"

"I think you know, Brian. You just don't want to admit it."

"I don't remember asking for advice, *Father*," Brian pointed out, feeling his temper spike.

"You're right," Liam said and he smiled again, even wider this time, as if to prove to both of them that Brian's temper didn't worry him. "But consider this a freebie." He leaned forward, forearms on the table and stared steadily into Brian's eyes. "You're not avoiding Tina for her sake, Brian. You're doing it for your own. You're hiding from her because you don't want to admit that you never should have let her go."

"Bullsh—"

"Ah," Liam said grinning, "fascinating, well-thought-out argument."

Brian huffed out a breath, dug in his pockets for his car keys, then glared at the booth full of Reillys. "You guys are making me even more nuts than Tina!"

He stomped off, and after a second or two, Aidan held up one hand toward the waitress and silently ordered another round of beers for the table. Then he glanced first at Connor, then at Liam. "Brian's a dead man," he said, smiling.

"Oh, yeah," Connor said, "a goner."

"I'll drink to that," Liam said and lifted his beer. "A toast. To Brian. May Tina make him suffer before taking him back."

"Amen."

"Ooh-rah."

Tina sat on the edge of the bathtub in the tiny bathroom, dressed only in a towel and reminded herself that this was what she'd come home for. Since she'd first hit town, Tina had started off every day the very same way—taking her temperature. And every day, she'd waited, wondering if this was the optimum day for conception or not. Then every day, she'd faced a mixture of disappointment mingled with relief.

Until today.

She pulled in a deep breath and let it slide from her lungs in a slow rush. Nerves twisted in the pit of her stomach, but she resolutely squashed them. Her temperature was right. Her eggs were ready. The time was now. If she was going to do this, she'd never have a better day than today.

And if she was a little nervous about the romantic ambush she'd been forced to plan, well, that was Brian's fault. He'd been sneaking into his apartment and sneaking out again in the mornings, avoiding her at all costs. "So what other choice did I have?" she asked, more to hear the sound of her own voice in the stillness of the apartment than anything else.

She crossed her legs, uncrossed them, then crossed them again in the other direction. Her stomach twisted and pitched and every nerve ending in her body seemed poised for panic.

"Silly." She muttered the word aloud, as if to convince herself. "This is Brian. We were *married* for Pete's sake. It's not like we've never—" her voice droned off into silence as memories, old and new, flooded her brain.

Of course, there were the memories of she and Brian, first married, and loving each other so desperately, so frantically, they could barely stand to be separated from each other. Then there were the long, empty years and then—images of the other night crowded her brain and Tina's stomach twisted again. This time from need. From want.

Brian had pushed her higher and faster than anyone else ever had and the crashing climax she'd found in his arms had only fed her hunger for more. She wanted his hands on her. She wanted to feel the rush and roar of her own blood racing through her veins.

And she wanted a baby.

Her head snapped up as a slight sound reached her. The front door of the apartment had opened.

Standing up, Tina smoothed her palms over the pale blue towel knotted between her breasts and falling to the tops of her thighs. She soothed her stomach with a deep gulping breath of air, then pulled open the bathroom door and stepped out.

Brian's gaze locked with hers.

His mouth fell open.

Tina smiled. "Surprise."

Seven

Brian just stared at her.

He tried to talk, but his throat closed up tight.

He'd been thinking about her all the way home from the restaurant. Liam's words had rattled around inside his brain until Brian was forced to wonder if maybe his big brother was right. But if Liam *was* right, then that meant that Brian had wasted five years of his and Tina's lives. So, his brother wasn't right, Brian told himself. Liam didn't realize that Brian had only divorced Tina to protect her. To save her years of misery.

Sure he regretted letting her go.

Never more than right now.

The old-fashioned wooden clock on the wall ticked loudly, sounding like a much steadier heartbeat than Brian's at the moment. Moonlight filled the shadowy room, streaming in the front windows like a silvery fog. Lamplight from the bathroom behind her, backlit Tina, defining her outline with a glow that was almost otherworldly.

But she was all too real.

And Brian was a doomed man.

Every inch of him went on red alert. He felt like he was strapped into a jet, parked on a carrier, readying himself for the roar of engines and the heart-stopping jolt of takeoff. Adrenaline pumped and his blood raced.

A second later, Tina started talking, and he fought the hunger to pay attention.

"…I locked myself out of Nana's house after my shower—"

He held up one hand for quiet. "You went outside dressed like that?" he managed to croak, and wondered if the fact that he found that idea incredibly sexy was a sign that he was truly twisted.

She smiled, slowly, wickedly. "I'm perfectly decent," she said. "Not like I went for a walk down Main Street. Besides, it's a big towel."

Not big enough, Brian thought frantically. She looked…beautiful. And edible. And irresistible. And so many other things, he could hardly name them all.

Her dark, curly hair brushed her shoulders, and her darker eyes glittered with expectation and a hunger he remembered only too well. His fingers itched to explore the length of her tanned, smooth legs and when she smiled, her lips looked full and luscious.

Then his gaze locked on the towel, knotted between her breasts. His breath hitched. Was the knot slipping?

Please.

Slip.

"Anyway," Tina said and strolled—there was no other word for it—*strolled* to the double bed on one side of the room and sat down on the edge. He swallowed hard as that towel edged apart slightly and rode high—too high—on her thighs. "I know you have a spare key for Nana's place and I didn't think you'd mind if I waited for you up here."

He watched her and wondered if she'd sat just there on purpose. Moonlight played over her, gilding her in a soft silver glow that made her even more beautiful than usual.

"No. Don't mind," he ground out and swallowed hard. His brain was clouding over. Not good. His body was pumped and eager. Also not a good thing.

Tina scooted around until she was stretched out on the bed, long legs crossed at the ankle, her back against the headboard. The moonlight loved her. As he watched, she lifted both arms and stretched lazily, as if she didn't have a care in the world. As if she wasn't nearly buck naked in *his* bed.

As if she wasn't driving him crazy with a wild desire that had a stranglehold on him.

"It's a nice apartment," she said, letting her gaze slide around the small room.

Now she's making small talk? he thought furiously. He was a man on a knife's edge and she wanted to talk about home furnishings? Bullshit. She was playing this out, deliberately torturing him. She knew what she was doing and knew what it was doing to him. No way was she actually admiring his place. He knew exactly what she was seeing. The studio apartment was small, efficient and anything but homey. But it had always suited him fine.

Until now.

Now, he didn't think the place would be big enough if it were a castle.

He'd still be able to smell her perfume.

Okay, key to his survival here, was to get Tina the hell out of his place as fast as possible. Preferably, without touching her or smelling her hair or…hell. *Anything.*

"C'mon," he said, grabbing up his keys and shifting his gaze away from her. There'd be no help for him at all if he kept looking at her. "I'll take you downstairs and let you in."

"What's your hurry?"

He looked.

She turned slowly onto her side.

Brian stifled a groan, but it almost killed him.

Head propped up in one hand, Tina kept her gaze locked on him as with her free hand, she inched the hem of the towel up a little higher on her thigh.

His heart pounded in his chest. He forgot how to breathe. His eyes glazed over.

And then the towel parted. One half of the pale blue terry cloth fell away, displaying a tantalizing slice of Tina's naked, curvy body to perfection.

Brian groaned. "You're killing me."

"*So* not what I had in mind," Tina said softly, making no move at all to cover herself.

He scraped one hand across his face, frantically trying to get a grip. And losing. "Your towel fell."

"I know."

"I know you know." Damn it. Why was she doing this? Was this a game? Payback maybe, for him getting the divorce? But if that's all it was, why wait five years to claim it?

And if it was more, what did that mean?

And if he asked himself any more questions, that didn't have answers, he really would slip over the edge into insanity.

"This is nuts," he blurted.

"Maybe."

His gaze locked with hers, studiously avoiding noticing her bare, beautiful skin. "You'll be sorry."

Tina smiled and shook her head. "Not if you're as good as I remember."

Like a punch to his gut, her words hit him hard and left him shaky. He was only human, right? Mere mortal? And faced with Tina Coretti, Brian was willing to guess there wasn't a man alive who could have walked out that door.

Still, he had one last hope. "I, uh…don't have any condoms here." Actually, he'd gotten rid of his stash purposely, since he figured with the bet on, keeping a supply handy would only submarine his chances of winning.

She smiled again. "Doesn't matter."

"Uh, yeah," he said tightly. "It does."

"Brian," she said, her voice dropping to a husky note that damn near killed him, "as long as you don't have some socially icky disease, you don't have to worry."

Don't have to worry. So she was on the pill. Okay, there went the last wall standing between him and glory.

It didn't matter anymore why she was here or what she wanted. Maybe it never had. Maybe since the day she arrived in Baywater, they'd been heading right here. To this place. Maybe it was something they both needed.

She trailed her fingertips up, over her hip, pushing the other half of the towel aside.

His mouth went dry.

His heart hammered in his chest.

"So?" she asked, her voice a whisper in the moonlight as she repeated her earlier question. "*Are* you as good as I remember?"

Even a Marine knew when to surrender.

Brian grinned and pulled off his shirt. "Babe. I'm *way* better."

She held one hand out to him. "Prove it."

He tore off his clothes, and in seconds, he was there, beside her on the bed. He peeled the towel off her body, then cupped one of her breasts.

"Brian…" she whispered, arching into him, pushing herself into his touch, "I want you so badly."

"I want you too, baby," he murmured, dipping his head to taste her nipple. A lick, a nip of his teeth and his words muffled against her flesh. "I've always wanted you."

She put her hands at the sides of his face and tipped his head up until she could look into his eyes. Brian read the hunger in those dark chocolate eyes of hers and something more. Something he didn't want to think about. Or acknowledge.

She pulled him close and kissed him, nibbling at his bottom lip for a long moment before saying, "Then take me, Brian. Take me and let me take you."

He was lost.

Groaning, he covered her mouth with his and swept his tongue into her warmth. Grabbing her tightly, he held her close, and took everything she had to give. His tongue mated with hers and his breath filled her as she filled him. He felt the heat of her, pressed along his body and thought wildly that he'd been so cold for five years. So damn cold and he'd never realized that it was because he didn't have her.

She was the heat.

The light.

Tina Coretti was the missing piece in his life and even if it was for this one night, it was good to have her back. To feel the connection blistering between them. To realize that here, at least, there was nothing else in the world that mattered. Here there was only the two of them and the magic they created together.

She moved against him, and slid her hands up and down his back, scoring his flesh with long swipes of her short, neat nails. And he wanted more. He wanted her to somehow mark him permanently, so that he would always carry a reminder of this night. This moment.

His brain raced, blood pumped and an ache he hadn't known in five long years built within. Sweeping one hand down the length of her body, he defined every curve, every line of her. He touched, caressed, explored. He tasted, as he shifted over her, trailing his lips and tongue along the line already drawn by his hands. She moved in his grasp, wriggling and sighing softly into the night.

And no music had ever sounded sweeter.

He ached for her.

Sliding down her length, he kissed every inch of her as he moved along her body. She lifted her hips, arching into him, digging her head deeper into the pillow beneath her. Her fingertips scraped across his shoulders as she reached for him, but he evaded her touch, determined now to explore all of her. To rediscover every hidden delight. To touch her as he had before—and as he'd dreamed of doing since.

"Brian," she whispered throatily, "I need you inside me."

"Not yet, babe," he answered, then nibbled at her abdomen, making her hiss in a breath. "Not yet."

Tina didn't think she could stand much more. Oh, she'd thought herself prepared. Thought that she remembered what it was like, being with Brian. Being the sole focus of his attentions.

But she hadn't.

It was so much more than mere memory could provide. The sensations coursing through her ebbed and flowed and rose up again, nearly swamping her with their strength. Her mind fogged over and her heartbeat tripped and staggered. Breathing was almost impossible. She couldn't think clearly enough to draw a breath—only remembering when she was on the verge of passing out from lack of air. Her vision swam and silvered in the moonlight and she lifted her head from the pillow to look down at the man moving over her.

She reached for him again, but he shifted, sliding around and down the front of her as though he were determined to taste every square inch of her body. She felt the fluttering nips and licks of his tongue and teeth and she shivered in his grasp.

Oh, she hadn't counted on this, Tina thought wildly, frantically as his hands moved over her hips, her thighs, exploring, defining. Then he was kneeling between her legs and Tina sucked in a gulp of air like a dying woman hoping for five last seconds of life.

"Brian—" she reached for him.

"Shut up, Coretti," he said, smiling, then scooped his hands beneath her bottom and lifted her hips off the mattress.

Tina grabbed fistfuls of the quilt beneath her and held on. He held her suspended, then deliberately hooked her legs over his shoulders and Tina watched him as he lowered his head and took her.

His mouth covered her, his lips and tongue did incredible things to flesh suddenly extremely sensitive. She held on tightly, fingers cramping in the fragile quilt fabric. The world tilted and only Brian's grip on her behind held her steady.

She couldn't look away. Her gaze locked on him.

He swiped her center with a long stroke of his tongue then nibbled at her core, and Tina groaned, rocking her hips into him, following the rhythm of his touch. She staggered toward a release that hung just out of reach and with every intimate caress, Brian pushed her higher, further.

Her breathing quickened and she reached for him again, and threaded her fingers through his hair as she held him to her. Kept his talented mouth in place as her body quickened and raced toward completion.

And when she screamed his name, she let herself fall, knowing that he held her safely.

Seconds trembled past and she shivered again, then opened her eyes to find him watching her, hunger dazzling his eyes. Slowly, he eased her back down onto the mattress, then moved to cover her body with his.

"I've really missed you, Tina," he said, dropping a soft kiss at the corner of her mouth.

"Oh, Brian, it's been too long." Her hands swept up and down his back, sliding over the familiar as though it were new.

"Don't think about that now," he said, frowning as he bent to kiss her once, twice. "Don't think at all."

"Don't give me time to think," she said and lifted her arms to encircle his neck, holding him tight, welcoming him with her body as well as her words. Welcoming him with everything she had. Everything she was.

He entered her body on a sigh and she felt—for the first time in far too long—*complete*.

Instantly, they were caught up in the rhythm. The slap of flesh to flesh, the thunder of hearts beating in time and the desire that pulsed around them, drawing them closer and uniting them into a single unit— as it always had.

Tina held on to him, lifting her legs, locking them around his hips and holding him tight, pulling him in deeper. Rocking her hips in time with his, she followed the frantic pace he set and gave herself up to the wonder of being in his arms again.

Her body quickened, sparkling with a renewed need that Brian hurried to meet. He thrust in and out of her heat, claiming and reclaiming all that had once been his. And she felt the strength of what they'd had and lost shimmering in the moonlight around them.

Her heart ached as her body sang and all Tina could do was hold him, cradle his body within hers and make these moments with him a memory that would sustain her long after she went home.

As the first tremors rocked her, Tina held him even tighter and raced with him to a climax that shook the foundations of everything they most believed. And as his body emptied into hers, she heard him whisper her name like a prayer.

"Damn it."

Tina tipped her head back on the pillow of his

chest and looked up at him. Smiling, she ran the tips of her fingers across his broad chest and said, "Not exactly the reaction most women look for after incredible sex."

"Incredible, huh?" His mouth twitched, then a heartbeat later, he was scowling. "That's not what I meant."

"Well," she said, turning into him and sliding up the front of his body in a deliberately slow, sinuous move, she brushed her hardened nipples against his chest. "Then I don't want to talk about whatever you *do* mean. Not now, anyway."

"No, we have to talk about this...." His voice trailed off as she slid slowly back down his body, trailing kisses and long swipes of her tongue over his flesh as she went. "Tina, cut it out."

She smiled against his abdomen. "You don't really want me to stop, do you?" she teased and shifted even lower.

"Yes—no—"

"Well, that's clear." Tina couldn't let him talk. Not now. She didn't want him regretting what they'd done because she wanted to do it again. And again. And again.

And not just because she wanted his baby growing inside her.

She did.

But more than that, she wanted Brian's *body* growing inside her, filling her, pushing her to heights she'd never reached with anyone else. She wanted him to want her as much as she did him.

She wanted him to *love* her as she did him.

That thought crashed through her mind and she at last admitted the plain, pitiful truth.

She'd never stopped loving her husband.

She'd never gotten over Brian Reilly.

And she didn't want to try.

That's why she wanted his child. If she couldn't have him in her life, she at least wanted a *part* of him to love.

"You're distracting me," he muttered.

"Good," she said and lifted her head long enough to smile at him. Then she bent and kissed his hard flesh, stroking the sensitive tip of him with her tongue. He gasped, dragging air into his lungs.

"Still distracted?" she asked.

"Come here," he demanded and sitting up, reached for her, dragging her along his body until he could flip her onto her back on the mattress. He kissed her, taking her mouth, stealing her breath, giving her his. His tongue met hers in a tangled dance of promise.

"No more talking."

"Who wants to talk?" she countered, grabbing at his shoulders, pulling him close. This is what she'd missed, she thought wildly. Being a part of Brian's life. Being able to turn to him in the night and find this warmth, this need, this hunger for her.

How she'd missed Brian.

She parted her legs for him and he moved quickly, eagerly, to enter her again. As if he couldn't bear another moment apart from her. Tina took him inside and felt the first staggering blasts of reaction dazzling within. He moved, his hips rocking, and sent waves of dizzying pleasure surging through her.

Tina planted her feet on the mattress and rocked hard against him, taking him deeper, higher inside. She moved, and he tormented. His mouth continued its tender assault on hers and as their bodies mated, they clung together, each taking something of the other.

He groaned and Tina swallowed the sound, burying it deep within. The first tiny tremors shook her as they built to an all encompassing finale and as Brian's body tightened, she held him to her, and this time, they took the fall together.

Eight

The rest of the night passed in a glorious haze of passion. Minutes crawled past and bled into hours that swept them both along on memories and a rush of desire that had been dammed up too long.

Dawn was just tracking colorful fingers across the horizon when Tina stretched, yawned and turned her head to glance out the window.

Every square inch of her body felt thoroughly used. Brian hadn't missed a trick and had, in fact, picked up a few new ones since the last time they'd been together. If her heart ached a little at the knowledge that he'd undoubtedly been with other women since they'd separated, she wouldn't let him know it.

She would bury that ache and keep it to herself. After all, she hadn't exactly lived like a nun for the past five years either.

But she was honest enough to admit, at least to herself, that no one had ever touched her the way Brian did. With another man, it was simply sex. With Brian, it was lovemaking that bordered on the spiritual.

She shifted her gaze back to him and smiled. Even sleeping, Brian didn't look innocent. He looked—*dangerous*. And he was. At least to her sense of well-being.

But with his dark blue eyes closed, she could indulge herself by studying him as she would any other gorgeous work of art. His chest rippled with muscles tanned to a deep, rich brown, despite his Irish heritage. A scattering of black hair swept down the center of his chest and disappeared beneath the pale green sheet they'd at last crawled under sometime during the night. One arm cocked behind his head, he slept with a smile on his face and damned if it wasn't an arrogant, self-satisfied smirk.

But, since she knew a like smile was currently curving her own mouth, she couldn't really blame him for it. One night with Brian was better than a hundred nights with anyone else. And how sad for Tina to discover that truth only to have to leave him again.

Hopefully though, this time when they parted, she would take a small piece of him with her. She dropped one hand to her abdomen and spread her fingers wide across it, as if already cradling the minute child that might be within.

"When a woman smiles like that," Brian said softly, "makes a man wonder what she's thinking about."

Tina started, then guiltily moved her hand from her belly to reach for the sheet, pulling it up to cover her breasts. "Um…"

He grinned. "Good answer." Then he turned onto his side, swept the sheet aside and cupped one of her breasts in his palm.

Tina sucked in a breath as his thumb and forefinger teased and tweaked her nipple.

"You're not feeling shy all of a sudden, are you?" Brian asked.

"No," she said, "just a little tired."

"Not surprising," he admitted. "Even I usually require more than an hour's sleep at night."

But that's all they'd had, she realized. Because neither of them had wanted to stop touching the other long enough to snooze, however briefly. Finally, exhaustion had slapped them both into sleep just before dawn.

When she didn't answer, his hand on her breast stilled and his gaze narrowed on her. "Are you all right?"

"Sure," she said, biting back her second thoughts, tamping down on the first stirring of guilt that was already beginning to nibble at the edges of her conscience.

"Yeah," he said, sitting up to look down at her. "I'm convinced."

The back of his neck itched.

Just like it did whenever he was in the field. Even at thirty thousand feet above the earth, a pilot could sense when there were missiles targeting his ship. And it was that very sixth sense that was jangling inside him now like a mission bell blowing in a hurricane wind.

"It's nothing, Brian. Really."

"It's something," he countered and told himself that he was pretty sure he wasn't going to like it. All night, he and Tina had connected just like the old days. Despite the lack of sleep tugging at him, he'd never felt more alive than he had at this moment. And he knew without a doubt that once Tina started talking, that well-being was going to fly out a window. And still, he had to *know*. "Why don't you just spill it?"

"I don't think that's a good idea," she said.

"Now I know we've gotta talk," Brian told her and felt his stomach clench into fists of anxiety. Something was definitely up.

"Let's not do this, okay?" she said and abruptly scooted to the edge of his bed and scrambled around on the floor, looking for the towel she'd discarded the night before.

"Okay, when Tina Coretti doesn't want to talk,"

Brian muttered darkly, "there's trouble. And I want to know what it is."

She shot him a look over her shoulder, blew her hair out of her eyes and gave him what she no doubt hoped would look like an innocent shrug.

"No trouble. Really. Just looking for a shower and some clothes now." She didn't want to have this talk now. Not when she knew it would lead to an argument of apocalyptic proportions. And Tina wasn't sure she was ready for that. Not when her body was still humming from his touch and her heart was still aching with the knowledge that she loved a man who didn't want her.

Where did the stupid towel go? she wondered. Not like it could walk off on its own.

"Why don't I believe you?"

She glanced at him again, tugged the sheet with her, draping it around her body before dropping to the floor. "Beats me," she said. "Maybe you have a suspicious nature?"

"Talk to me, Tina," he complained and she heard the impatience in his voice and winced at it.

So much for the happy afterglow thing, she thought as she continued to grope her way across the floor, looking under tables and the edge of the bed for her wayward towel. "You know what?" She staggered to her feet, caught her toe on the hem of the sheet and stumbled forward a step or two. "Screw the towel. I'll just borrow this sheet to go back to Nana's house in. I'll bring it back to you tonight."

Then she made the mistake of turning around to look at him. Naked and comfortable with it, he was sprawled across the rumpled sheets, braced on his elbows as he watched her. Every square inch of him was gorgeous. He looked like a statue carved by a master craftsman. Well, except for the suspicion gleaming in his eyes.

"Not a chance," he muttered.

"You don't trust me with your *sheet*?"

"I don't give a good damn about the stupid sheet, Tina," he said, sliding off the bed and stalking toward her. "I want to know what's going on inside that head of yours and you're not leaving until you tell me."

Tina took an instinctive step backward, then stiffened her spine and stood her ground. After all, she wasn't ashamed of what she'd done. Well, not totally, anyway. It wasn't as if she'd had to hold a gun to his head to get him to have sex with her, right? He'd enjoyed himself. *Many* times.

Although, said a little voice in the back of her mind, *if he'd known what you were doing, he never would have slept with you.*

But then, she reasoned, however faulty, that's precisely why she hadn't told him.

Until now.

She forced herself to look into his eyes, because

looking anywhere else would only send her blood into a frothing rush—and she knew darn well that once he knew what was going on…there wouldn't be any more rolling around on those rumpled sheets.

Their gazes locked and Brian studied her features for what felt like forever. Then slowly, her gaze shifted to one side as if she couldn't quite look him in the eyes. Not a good sign.

"Last night," he said, his voice low and dangerous, "when you said I didn't have to worry about not having condoms…"

Tina reached up and pushed her hair back from her face. With her free hand, she clutched the sheet to her chest like some ancient battle shield. "Yes?"

"You *did* mean that you were on the pill, right?"

"Not exactly."

His features froze over. Some unidentifiable emotion—panic maybe, or fear—clawed at his chest. She still wouldn't look directly at him. Oh yeah, his sixth sense was never wrong.

"Not *exactly*?" he repeated, remembering just how many times he'd made love to Tina during the night. How many times his little warriors had stormed her undefended beaches. The air in the room got a little thin and he had to gulp in oxygen like a drowning man. "Just what the hell does 'not exactly' mean?"

"It means that I'm not on the pill, but you don't have to worry."

Not on the pill.

Four words guaranteed to strike fear into the hearts of men everywhere. The world shifted just a bit and he felt as though he were perched on the edge of a cliff and already sliding swiftly toward a crevasse that was going to swallow him whole. And there wasn't a damn thing he could do about it.

Don't have to worry? he thought. What the hell kind of man did she think he was? Did she really believe he could make a child and walk away? Didn't she know him at all?

Oh, God.

A baby?

His blood pumped and the furious roaring in his ears sounded a backdrop for the bass drum beating of his heart.

"And I shouldn't worry because…"

Here it comes. Tina had known all along that she'd have to tell him. That she wouldn't be able to *not* tell him. But it was different, now.

Back home in California, when she was talking to Janet, planning all of this, thinking it through, she'd done it objectively. She'd reasoned it all out and the plan had seemed fair to her. She would have the child she'd always wanted and Brian would have the opportunity to either be a part of the child's life or not, as he chose.

Now though, guilt was a living thing inside her.

Now, she regretted the lie to him—though she didn't regret her actions, not one bit. She wouldn't trade the past several hours with Brian for anything. And hopefully, they'd created a child—and she would love it with all her heart.

The problem was, she loved Brian, too. And loving him, she could feel badly for tricking him into this. For taking advantage of the nearly magical chemistry they'd always shared. But if she had to live with guilt to have his child, then that's just the way it would have to be.

She looked up at him and etched this image of him into her brain. Stern, his face set in hard planes and sharp angles, his eyes glittering with impatience and the first stirring of temper. Outside, the sun was creeping into the sky, sending the first pale rays of light reaching into the shadows of the room. Birds chirped, the wind blew softly and the day moved forward even while time seemed to click to a standstill here in Brian's apartment.

He reached for her, his hands coming down on her shoulders, his fingers digging into her flesh, branding her skin with heat. "Tell me what the hell you think you're doing, Tina. I've got a right to know."

She steadied herself, taking a deep breath and blowing it out again before trying to answer him. Then tossing her hair behind her shoulders, she looked him dead in the eye and started talking. "Yes, you do. And I was going to tell you anyway, I want you to know that."

"Tell me *what*?"

"That I want to be pregnant."

He blinked, opened his mouth, then slammed it shut again, clearly waiting for more.

She gave it to him.

"And I'm really hoping that we made a baby last night."

He let her go so suddenly, she staggered backward a step or two before regaining her balance. His eyes went wide and he looked at her as if she were a stranger who'd wandered into his room accidentally.

"A *baby*?"

Tina winced slightly at the horrified tone in his voice, but she stood her ground defiantly. A Coretti didn't hide from responsibility. "That's right. I wanted a baby and I wanted you to be the father."

He reached up and shoved both hands along his skull, as if he were trying to keep his brain from exploding. "*You* wanted," he said after a long, painful moment of silence. "You didn't think I should get a vote in that?"

Tina's lips quirked and her gaze slid past him to the bed and back again. "You voted yes, Brian. Many times as I recall."

"I voted for *sex*," he pointed out harshly. "Don't remember voting for *fatherhood*."

That stung and because it was true, she only nodded. "I know. But when I said you didn't have to worry, I meant it."

"Right. Don't worry. Make babies, move on."

"Brian, I *want* this baby."

"Don't say that," he snapped. "We don't know that there *is* a baby."

She slapped one hand to her abdomen, as if she could block the ears of the microscopic life that might already be forming inside her. "I hope to heaven there is."

"Tina, what in the hell were you thinking?"

"I just told you."

"Uh-huh," he muttered thickly and moved past her, grabbing up his jeans and tugging them on. "Your biological clock ticks and the alarm goes off on *me*?"

"For God's sake, Brian," she said, gathering up her sheet and holding it even tighter around her body, "you don't have to act like I pulled a gun on you and *forced* you to have sex with me."

His head snapped up and he pinned her with a look that would have terrified a lesser woman. But Tina was used to the Reilly temper. And had one of her own to match.

"You tricked me," he said.

"I tempted you," she corrected, clinging to that distinction.

"You knew damn well what you were up to and didn't tell *me*."

"Oh, please," she said, pushing her stupid hair back out of her eyes again. He was dressed now. So unfair. He had the advantage here. Hard to fight for your rights with dignity when you're wearing a pale green toga. "Don't act like some poor little virgin who was taken advantage of. You were more than willing, thanks to that idiotic bet you and your brothers made."

He stopped. "You know about the bet?"

"Yep."

He scowled. "Liam."

"Yep."

He lifted one finger and pointed it at her like a physical accusation. "So you set this up deliberately. You caught me at a weak moment."

One dark eyebrow lifted. "And your point is?"

Furious now, Brian buttoned up his jeans, planted both hands at his hips and glared at her. "You should have told me."

All of the air left her lungs in a rush and she almost felt like a balloon deflating in the hands of a greedy child. Hindsight was always twenty-twenty, she reassured herself. And he might have a tiny, tiny, point. "Maybe."

"No maybe about it, babe."

Tina winced. Funny. He'd called her "babe" all

night and it had sounded sexy, titillating. Now it sounded cold and dismissive. "If I'd told you, you wouldn't have cooperated."

"Hah!" He grinned victoriously. "Exactly my point."

Sighing now, Tina felt regret pool in her stomach and spread cold tentacles throughout her body. How sad it was, she thought, that the two of them had come to this. How sad that so much fire was now only an empty chill in a shadowy room. "Brian, I don't want anything from you."

"No, why should you?" He threw both hands high and let them slap down against his thighs again. "You've already gotten what you needed from me."

From outside, the roar of a jet streaking by overhead thundered through the room and Tina felt a hard jolt. Soon enough, she'd be home again in California, alone, and praying for the existence of the child Brian didn't want. And Brian would be here, flying those jets, preparing to step back into danger at a moment's notice.

She'd thought she could come into town, sleep with Brian and make a baby, then slip right back into her world. But the truth was, she would never really be free of Brian. It was the plain and simple truth.

No wonder none of the men she'd dated over the years had been able to touch her heart. Her heart had always been here, in Baywater with her ex-husband.

She couldn't fall in love with anyone else when she still loved Brian Reilly.

As if he, too, felt the sense of misery creeping into her heart, he said, with regret rather than temper, "Don't you get it, Tina? I don't want to be a part-time father."

"You don't have to be, Brian," she said and wondered if he knew what it cost her to say this. "I'm not asking you to be an active parent. You can be as involved or as distant as you choose to be."

"Oh," he said quietly, "*now* I get a vote?"

"Yes," she said, just as quietly, "when I told you not to worry, I meant it. If you want to, you can never speak to me again."

"Just like that."

Okay, she was willing to admit that maybe, *maybe,* what she'd done had been a mistake. Unfair to him. But she wasn't going to stand here and let him pretend that he'd rather things were different between them. "Yes, Brian. Just like that. It's been five years, remember? And we've talked maybe three times in all that time."

"This is different," he snarled. "What's between you and I is one thing. What's between me and a child I created, is something else altogether. You think I could let my child not be a part of my life?"

"That'll be up to you."

"Gee, thanks."

Despite the already growing heat, Tina felt a chill snake along her spine and she wished fervently that they'd never had this conversation. She should have waited to see if there was a baby before confronting him with the possibilities.

"There's no point in talking about this anymore," she said suddenly, turning as she spoke to head for the door. "I'm going back to the house."

"What about locking yourself out?" he said, sarcasm dripping from every word.

She stopped, one hand on the doorknob, and shot him a look over her shoulder. "I lied."

"Big surprise."

Her shoulders hunched as his words slapped at her. "I'm sorry you're mad, Brian," she said, never taking her gaze from his, despite inwardly flinching from the fury she saw written in his eyes. "But I'm not sorry about last night. And I'm not sorry that we might have made a baby." She opened the door and paused again. "I am sorry that you are, though."

Then she stepped through the door and closed it softly behind her.

Brian stood alone in the growing patch of sunlit warmth and had never felt so bone-deep cold in his life.

Nine

Later that morning, Brian really lived up to his call sign, Cowboy. Every pilot had his own nickname used during flights. Some of his best friends were known as Bozo, or Too Cool, or Goliath. Brian though, had come by his call sign because of his aggressive approach to flying.

Nothing he liked better than doing loops and spins miles above the ground. Ordinarily, too, he emptied his mind of everything but the task at hand—much safer to be thinking *only* about flying when you went faster than the speed of sound.

But today, Tina was flying with him.

She was there beside him in the close confines of

the cockpit. She was in his blood, in his brain, and to get her out again, was going to be far tougher than anything he'd ever faced before.

"She *tricked* me," he muttered, still unable to grasp the fact that his ex-wife had deliberately set him up to father her child.

"What?" The voice came from the seat behind him. His radar officer, Sam "Hollywood" Holden.

"Nothin'."

"Okay, Cap'n," Hollywood said, "that's the way you want it. So if you're finished trying to make me upchuck my breakfast, why don't we turn this puppy around and head home?"

Brian grinned. "What's wrong, Hollywood? Late night last night?"

"Hey," his friend pointed out with a chuckle. "Not all of us signed up for that stupid bet."

Groaning, Brian shook his head and stared into the clouds whizzing past the plane. Impossible to keep a secret on a military base. At least *this* kind of secret. Spies, battle plans, sure. You were safe. A humiliating, personal problem—fair game.

He never should have agreed to the bet. If he had told Liam to get lost, he never would have been in such a vulnerable condition when Tina hit town. And he never would have spent a long, endless night exploring her body.

Hard to regret that, even considering the way it had ended.

However, he'd be damned if he'd just sit back and let the guys get a good laugh at his expense.

"Just for that," Brian said with an evil chuckle, already maneuvering his jet into an upside-down position, "I think we'll just fly home inverted."

"Oh, *man....*"

"I really made a mess of this, didn't I?" Tina looked down at Muffin and Peaches, sprawled across her bed. "Not that I'm really regretting it. I mean, that *is* why I came here, right?"

Peaches yawned and rolled over.

Tina paced, marking off the same steps in her old room that she had as a teenager when she was angsting over the serious problems that had faced her back then. Things like, would she ever get her hair straightened? Would she ever get a date? Would she ever get out of AP Chem?

Well, times had changed and the problems had gotten bigger. But her solutions were still the same. Pace and talk to herself.

"It's not like I *forced* him, you know," she said aloud, shooting a look at Muffin, since Peaches, the little traitor, was snoring. "He was more than willing."

Muffin yapped.

"So why do I feel so blasted guilty?" she demanded and knew the answer, though she didn't really want to look at it too closely. Using Brian had been wrong. "Fine. I'm a rotten human being. Stand me up against a wall and shoot me." She stopped at the foot of the bed and plopped down onto the edge of the mattress. "I just wanted—"

What? A baby? Sure. But that wasn't all, was it? No. She'd wanted Brian back. She hadn't been able to admit it even to herself before she'd arrived back in Baywater. But it was impossible to deny now.

It wasn't just his child she wanted.

It was his heart.

And that was the one thing she couldn't have.

Pushing herself to her feet, Tina stalked around the edge of the bed, grabbed the phone and punched in a familiar number. It rang twice.

"Hello?"

"Janet." Tina sighed, reached down to scoot a limp Peaches over and then sat down. "Thank God."

"Tina! How's it going girl?"

"Not so good."

"Oh." Janet was silent for a long minute. "So you couldn't get him to—"

"No," Tina said, toying with the pale blue, coiled cord of the ancient Princess phone. "Mission accomplished."

A long pause. "Really? You mean you really went to bed with your ex?"

"No," Tina said, scooting back farther on the bed. "I asked him for a donation, then I took it to the clinic and had them douse me with a turkey baster."

Janet laughed. "Well, for someone who just had sex, you seem a little cranky."

Frowning, Tina said, "I'm sorry. I'm just mad at myself and you're easier to yell at."

"Happy to help."

"Janet, it didn't go like I thought it would."

"It wasn't as great as you remembered?"

"It was better."

"So what's the problem?"

"I told him." Tina closed her eyes and saw Brian's face again. The betrayal in his eyes and the fury stamped on his features. She couldn't really blame him. *He'd* divorced *her,* after all. And if he hadn't wanted her as his wife, why would he want her as the mother of his child? A child, by the way, he hadn't realized he'd been conceiving. Maybe.

"Ahh…" Janet's sigh was long and eloquent. "You knew going in he wouldn't be happy about it."

"I know," she said and shook her head even as she dropped one hand to Peaches's back and stroked the little dog gently. "But I didn't know I'd—"

"—still love him?" Janet finished for her.

"Well, yeah."

"Tina, honey, this way lies pain."

"You're right, but—" Tina's brain went back to the

night before. The passion, the desire, the hunger that had risen up and engulfed them both. It had been stronger somehow, *bigger* than what she and Brian had shared five years before. Was it because they'd been apart so long?

Or was it because they were meant to be together?

"So what are you going to do about it?"

Tina scowled. "What can I do?"

"Honestly, Tina," Janet said, clucking her tongue loud enough that it sounded as though she were right beside Tina instead of at home, more than three thousand miles from South Carolina. "You love him and you're just going to walk away again?"

Tina stiffened slightly. "I didn't walk the last time, remember? Brian did."

"And you let him decide for both of you what was going to happen."

"Yes, but—"

Janet didn't let her finish. "How about this time, the two of you actually *talk* about what happened?"

Good idea, in theory, Tina thought grimly. But as she remembered the look on Brian's face when she'd left his apartment only that morning, she had a feeling that he would be a little less than receptive.

"And say what?"

"I don't know," Janet said, sarcasm dripping from every word, "how about, *I love you?*"

Those three words echoed over and over again in

Tina's mind as she stared blankly out the window. Outside, sunset pulsed in the sky, gilding the cloud-streaked horizon in brilliant shades of crimson and lavender.

"I said that five years ago," Tina whispered, remembering the pain. "It didn't help."

"Couldn't hurt, either."

"Maybe," she said, then changed the subject abruptly. There were no easy answers here. Nothing had really changed between her and Brian. And though she loved him and probably always would, she wasn't going to tell Brian. What would be the point? Another chance at humiliation when he told her *again* that he didn't want to be married to her? No, she thought. Passion was one thing—love was another. And all during the long night with Brian, he'd never once mentioned love.

While Janet talked about her pregnancy and the plans she had for her baby, Tina kept one hand firmly atop her flat abdomen. Silently, she prayed that inside, a child was already beginning to grow.

And if she was lucky, a small part of Brian would always be a part of her life—and no one would be able to take that away from her.

"I'm out."

Connor, Aidan and Liam stared at Brian for a long minute. He shifted under that steady regard, then bounced the basketball a few times before turning, jumping and shooting for the basket. The ball ricocheted off the backboard and crashed through the pretty stretch of flowers lining the rectory's driveway.

"Perfect," he muttered. Couldn't even make a basket. When he snatched up the ball again, he turned to see his brothers still watching him, wide grins on their faces.

"You didn't even last a month," Connor pointed out.

"Pitiful," Aidan said and came toward him, grabbing the basketball and shooting, making a perfect *swish* through the net.

"What happened?" Liam asked.

Brian wiped sweat out of his eyes with his forearm, then squinted at his brother the priest. The backyard lights spilled onto the wide driveway, lighting up the makeshift basketball court where he and his brothers fought vicious games of two-on-two ball a couple of nights a week.

Brian snapped his fingers a couple of times. "Keep up, Liam. I said I'm out of the contest. Measure me now for the hula skirt and coconut bra."

"I love this," Aidan said, taking another shot. "I can already feel that money bulging in my wallet."

"Yeah?" Connor countered, making a jump for the ball as it rebounded, "don't start spending it yet, pal."

The two of them argued and fought for the ball as Liam strolled across the driveway toward Brian.

Scowling, Brian watched his brothers shooting hoops and listened to the metallic *twang* as the ball slapped against the rim with every shot. A full moon shone down from a clear night sky and the scent of jasmine floated on the thick, summer air.

"You don't look so good," Liam said.

"Told you," Brian snapped, giving his older brother a quick, heated glance, "I lost the bet."

"This isn't about the bet."

"Yeah? Then tell me, *Father,* what's it about?"

Liam smiled and shook his head as if he were watching a particularly stubborn five-year-old. "It's about Tina. And *you.*"

Thoughts, questions, doubts, nibbled at the edges of his mind, as they had all day. He'd gotten through work, but he'd avoided going home. He wasn't ready yet to face Tina. To look at her and remember the night before. To remember that she'd tricked him. That even now, his *child* might be nestled inside her body.

Brian's stomach twisted and a knot lodged in his throat. Wasn't sure what that meant, but he had an idea and he didn't want to acknowledge it. Even to himself.

"There is no me and Tina," he said softly.

"Maybe there should be," Liam told him, and turning, steered Brian farther down the driveway, away from Connor and Aidan's shouting. "Maybe you've been given a second chance, Brian."

"A chance to make a jackass of myself in a hula skirt?"

Liam shook his head. "This isn't about the bet, Brian. You're not paying attention." He stopped at the end of the driveway and took a long moment, to look up and down the street. From a distance, came the sounds of kids playing, a car engine firing up and a stereo system blasting out some classic rock and roll.

Smiling, Liam lifted one arm and pointed at the houses crouched behind ancient trees. "What do you see?"

Brian snorted. "Maple Street."

"And…?"

Blowing out a breath, Brian turned and looked. "Houses. Trees. Dogs."

"Families," Liam said. "Homes."

Brian scraped one hand across his jaw and narrowed his gaze. "What's your point, Liam?"

"How many of those families are military, do you think?"

"What difference does that make?"

"All the difference to some, none at all to others," Liam said.

"Are you a priest or Confucius? For God's sake, make your point."

"You're an idiot, Brian." Liam shoved his younger brother and watched him stagger before regaining his balance.

Brian instantly lifted both hands, curled into fists. "Hey, you wanna go a round or two, fine by me."

The streetlight nearby spotlighted them in a circle of white and cast deep shadows on Liam's face. But despite the shadows, Brian saw a look of utter disgust on his brother's features.

"I don't want to fight you," Liam snapped. "I'm trying to tell you that instead of being here, with us—" he waved one hand at the driveway behind him, indicating Aidan and Connor, still throwing hoops. "You should be back at Angelina's house, talking to Tina."

The urge to fight dissolved and Brian shifted his gaze to the street and the houses beyond. "We're done talking."

"Just like five years ago then, huh? Your way or nothing?"

"You don't know what you're talking about," Brian warned.

"I know you, Brian." Liam shook his head, clearly disgusted. "I know Tina was the best thing that ever happened to you. And I know you *loved* her and you were *happy* until you decided to chuck it all."

"My business."

"Undoubtedly. All I'm saying is that maybe fate just handed you a second chance and you'd be an idiot to turn your back on it."

"I didn't ask for a second chance."

"That's what makes you *lucky,* you moron."

Brian snorted. "Nice priestly manner."

"You want a priest?" Liam asked, already turning to head back to the game, "show up at Mass once in awhile. Here, all you'll get is a brother."

Brian stared after him for several long minutes. Absently, he listened to the sounds of his brothers laughing and talking trash. Then he turned his gaze on Maple Street. And for the first time, he really thought about something Liam had said.

Probably half of those tidy little houses with neat lawns and carefully tended flower beds were lived in by military families. Husband or wife—and sometimes both—lived their lives according to the Corps, going where they were told, when they were told, never sure if they were going to be coming back.

And yet…Brian listened to the sound of a dog's excited bark and a kid's delighted laughter, drifting to him on the summer breeze. Somehow, most of those families made it work for them.

Five years ago, he'd decided that he couldn't put Tina through the misery of a life dictated by military needs. He'd told himself at the time that it wasn't fair to her. Wasn't fair to expect her to pick up, pack up and move across the country, sometimes around the world, whenever his orders changed. It was too much to ask her to live alone for months at a time when he was deployed. He'd thought it wasn't right to keep her in a marriage where her husband had a damn good chance of never coming home at all.

And he'd let her go.

For her sake.

It had cost him everything to cut Tina out of his life. And he'd felt the hollow emptiness ever since.

Now that Tina was back, he felt that emptiness even more sharply. It was a razor, slicing his soul, tearing at his heart. She'd wanted a baby.

His baby.

And he wondered if he'd made a big mistake five years ago.

Was he really the moron Liam claimed?

Ten

Two days later, and Brian was still thinking. Not that it was doing him much good.

He'd been able to avoid Tina so far, but that couldn't last. His ex-wife was *not* a woman to be ignored. He smiled as he remembered just the night before, her footsteps pounding up the stairs to his apartment and her voice demanding that he open the door and talk to her.

Naturally, he hadn't. He'd only shouted at her to go away and she'd left. Eventually.

But he knew damn well this armed truce couldn't last.

He pulled into the driveway, casting a quick

glance around to make sure the coast was clear. Man, what was the world coming to when a *Marine,* for God's sake, was skulking in and out of his house to avoid a woman?

Twilight was just beginning to fall and the air was a bit cooler as a soft sigh of wind drifted in off the ocean. From down the street came the unmistakable scent of a barbecue being fired up and a couple of kids were tossing a baseball in the street. Situation normal.

So why did he feel as knotted up and wired as he did when about to fly a combat mission?

The answer to that question opened up the screen door and stepped onto the porch. The two dogs hot on her heels followed after, yapping and snarling as they pelted off the porch and across the yard toward him. Presumably, they were ready to chew on what was left of his sorry butt once Tina was through with him.

She had blood in her eye and an expression of fierce determination on her face as she marched toward him. Looked like his stalling time was up. Briefly, Brian considered firing up the engine, throwing the car into gear and roaring back out of the driveway. But that smacked just a little too much of retreat, so he ignored the urge and stepped out of the car.

On the street, the kids hooted and jeered at each other as the ball flew wildly. In the yard, Muffin and Peaches were headed directly toward Brian and he imagined they were looking at him like a giant chew toy.

Then one of the kids missed a catch and the baseball shot past him, landing in the yard and rolling fast toward the flower bed. Peaches shifted direction and took off after it as though it were a gazelle and she a mighty lion. Her little feet flew and her ears flapped. She was almost on the ball when one of the kids threw a rock, hit her on a hind leg and the dog dropped with a yelp.

"Hey!" Furious, Tina shifted direction, heading for the downed dog.

Scared, the kid started backing off, but Brian was already moving to intercept. Anger pulsed through him as he heard loud whimpers from the injured dog. God knew he and the little ankle biters weren't close friends, but he wouldn't stand for one of the little dogs being hurt.

He reached the kid in a few long strides and dropped both hands on the boy's shoulders. Couldn't have been more than ten, Brian thought and right now, he was looking scared enough to cry. Good.

"What the hell are you doing?" Brian demanded.

"It's my ball, is all," the boy said, shooting a glance at the dog now being petted and stroked by Tina, kneeling on the ground beside it.

"And you thought that little dog was going to eat it?" Brian demanded.

"No," he said, his voice hitching close to the same note as the dog's whimper.

"You threw a *rock* at a three-pound dog," Brian growled, using his best, put-the-fear-of-God-into-your-enemy voice.

"I didn't mean to hurt her…"

The kid's friend, Brian noted, had already deserted the field, scampering out of range of punishment or retribution. The boy still in his grasp was trembling and Brian, keeping a firm grip on one shoulder, steered him toward the yard. "What do you think your mom would have to say about you throwing rocks at animals?"

"Oh, *man*," the kid whined pitifully. "Don't tell her, okay? I'm really sorry. Honest I am. C'mon, mister, don't tell my mom."

Brian heard the desperation and could appreciate it. When he and his brothers were ten, there wasn't anything they wouldn't have done to get out of letting their parents know they'd screwed up. "All right, I won't. But, you're going to go check on that dog. Make sure she's all right. *Then* you're going to apologize to the lady. Then you can have your ball back."

The boy blew out a relieved breath, then ran the back of his hand under his nose and sniffed dramatically. Every step dragged through the grass as if it were thick mud, sucking him down. He kept his head lowered and shot a wary glance up at Brian before shifting his gaze to Tina.

"I didn't mean to hurt her," he said and his voice shook a little.

"Then you shouldn't have thrown a rock," she said tightly.

"I'm really sorry." He went down on one knee next to the little dog and petted her head gently. Looking at Tina he promised, "I won't ever do it again, I swear."

Tina glanced at Brian and he smiled, nodding. He figured the kid was scared enough to make good on his word. And after all, what kid *didn't* throw a rock at the wrong time at one point in his life?

"All right then," Tina said, as she watched Peaches lick the boy's hand. "If Peaches can forgive you, so can I."

"Thanks, lady," the boy said, reaching for his ball and standing up again. He lifted his chin and met Brian's steely stare with more courage than he'd shown before. "I *am* sorry, y'know."

"Yeah," Brian said, jerking his head toward the street. "Go on."

The kid ran—as if he might not get a second chance at escape. Brian watched him, baggy jeans, torn sneakers and faded T-shirt, as he sprinted for his own house and safety. And just for a minute, Brian wondered what it would be like to have a child of his own.

Which of course, brought him full circle, right back to where he'd started.

He thought about the night with Tina and the chances of their having made a baby. And for the first time, that possibility felt real. He could almost see the kid's face. A fascinating combination of his and Tina's features. Unexpectedly, a curl of something warm unwound inside him.

A baby.

Brian Reilly, *father*.

And the notion of that didn't seem as weird, or terrifying as it had a couple of days ago.

"Ooh," Tina said, "I wanted to shake him so badly."

"He's pretty shook already," Brian said, going down on one knee in the grass. "How's the dog?"

"She's all right," Tina said. "It wasn't a very big rock, thank heaven."

Muffin sidled up close to Brian and leaned into him. Without even thinking about it, he stroked her cream-colored curls. Peaches slipped out from under Tina's gentle hand and trotted to Brian, too. Planting both front feet on his knee, she sat down and stared up at him in adoration.

He looked down at the dogs who'd been the bane of his existence for years and couldn't believe it. Neither one of them was trying to go for his jugular.

"Looks like they're in love," Tina quipped.

Brian's gaze snapped to hers. "What?"

"You're their hero, apparently."

He frowned at the two tiny dogs.

They sighed.

"Oh, this is weird."

"You'd rather they were snarling at you?"

"At least I know what to expect then."

"And that's important?" Tina asked.

He looked at her again. "I don't like surprises."

"Brian—"

He cut her off. "Tina, I don't want to talk about it again."

"Again?" she countered. "We haven't talked about it *yet*."

Peaches tried to crawl up his body, so Brian gently picked her up and set her back down again. Muffin leaned harder against him.

Brian tried to ignore the dogs and focus on the woman watching him. He could already see the fires of indignation beginning to kindle in her eyes and he braced himself. "Fine. Can we at least take this inside?"

"You bet." She jumped to her feet, snapped her fingers and said, "C'mon, girls."

Neither dog moved.

"Muffin? Peaches?"

Brian scowled at the little animals.

They sighed.

He sighed, too, as he stood up and the dogs fell into step behind him. He headed for the front porch, ignoring the stupefied expression on Tina's face as he and his entourage walked to the house.

"I'm sorry I tricked you," Tina blurted the minute they were in the door.

"Old news," Brian said, walking past her to the

couch where he sat down and winced as both dogs jumped into his lap at once.

Tina frowned at the three of them. The dogs, the little traitors, had shifted their affections to him and she felt like a complete outsider, now. She buried the irritation and took a seat on the sofa opposite him.

"Old or not, I wanted you to know that I've thought about it and I realize that it was wrong of me to do it."

"Thanks," he said, shoving both dogs off his lap and leaning forward, his forearms on his knees. "But that doesn't change the fact that we have to deal with the consequences."

"So businesslike," she murmured, shaking her head. "Very admirable."

"Would you rather I shout and stomp around the room?"

"Actually?" she mused, "Yes."

"Already did that," he pointed out. "Didn't change anything."

"Look, Brian," she said, hating the calm, indifferent tone of his voice. She'd much rather have one of their legendary arguments. An Irish temper and an Italian temper could get pretty loud when they clashed. But the making up had always been worth the storm. "I meant what I said the other night. If I am pregnant—"

He winced and she tried not to notice.

"—then I'll deal with it myself. You don't have to—"

"Just stop right there," he demanded and shifted when Peaches made a try for his lap again. "If you're pregnant, then it's *our* baby and *we* deal with it."

"How do you mean *deal*?"

"Take care of it, of course. What the hell do you think I mean?" His temper spiked a little and Tina immediately felt better.

"I can raise a child, Brian," she said.

"Not my child. Not alone."

For one brief second, Tina entertained the notion that just maybe he'd missed her as much as she'd missed him. That maybe he was going to suggest that they might still work this out. That there was a future for the two of them after all.

And when that heartbeat of time passed, reality struck.

"I've been thinking about this," he said. "For two days now. And if you're pregnant, I can make arrangements."

Wary now, she asked, "What kind of arrangements?"

"Well," he said, in an abstracted tone, almost as if he were thinking aloud and didn't really like his thoughts very much. "I could leave the Corps. Take a civilian job. For one of the airlines."

"What?" Tina stood up and looked down at him. "You can't leave the Marines."

"I admit it's not my first choice, but—"

"Brian, don't be stupid. Being a Marine isn't your job. It's who you *are*."

Slowly, he pushed himself to his feet. "Tina—"

"No," she said, cutting him off before he could get started. "I would never ask you to leave the Corps. I know what it means to you. And I would never want you to be less than you are."

He pushed one hand along the side of his head. "Families are hard enough under the best of circumstances," he muttered. "But military families have a tougher road than most."

She stared at him as if she'd never seen him before. Where was this coming from?

"I've seen families splintered," he said tightly. "My friends, leaving their wives for months at a time. The spouse of a Marine gets all the crap jobs. Handling cross-country or around-the-world moves alone. Raising kids, paying bills, worrying about every damn thing all on their own." He started pacing and as he walked, the words bubbled up and out of him as if they'd been dammed up for way too long and just had to escape. "There's no one there to help, you know? It's hard. And that's not even counting all the worrying. Money's tight and housing stinks. You get deployed to danger zones all over the world and sometimes can't even tell your wife where the hell you are."

"Brian—" She stood stock still and followed him with her gaze.

He held up one hand and kept talking. "There's long hours and a lot of alone time. It's a hard life, and I wanted you to have better. I wanted you to be happy, and didn't want to think about you doing without or being alone or spending your whole damn life worrying about me and where I was and—"

Tina trembled. She felt twin waves of regret and fury rock through her as she listened to the man she loved tell her exactly why he'd ended their marriage five years before. He may have started out talking about their current situation, but she knew damn well, he'd somehow drifted back and was finally giving her the answers she'd wanted so badly five years ago.

Now that she had those answers though, she was furious.

"Are you telling me," she said, loudly enough to interrupt him at last, "that you divorced me because you wanted me to be *happy*?"

He stopped pacing and shot her a look. "Yes," he said. "I did it for you."

"You moron."

"You know," he said, every word ground out from between clenched jaws, "that's the second time this week somebody's called me a moron. Don't much like it."

"Don't much care," Tina snapped, stalking around the edge of the sofa to walk straight up to him. She stopped only inches from him and jabbed him in the chest with an index finger. "You divorced me for my own sake? *You* decided that I wouldn't be a good Marine wife?"

"That's not what I said—"

"It's exactly what you said," she cut him off again, and let herself go, riding the crest of the fury that was threatening to blow the top of her head clean off. "You thought I couldn't hack it. You thought I was too soft, or too weak or too stupid to be able to take care of myself while my big, strong husband was off protecting my country?"

"No…" Wariness tinged his voice.

"You thought I couldn't be trusted to raise our children, to pay some bills, to pack for a move, for heaven's sake?"

"I didn't—"

"You figured that without my husband standing close by, I'd curl up into a ball and cry?"

"Tina—"

"Did you really think so little of me?"

"I loved you."

"But obviously, you didn't *respect* me at all."

"Of course I did."

"If you did, you wouldn't have done this. Wouldn't have treated me like a child sent off to my room," she snapped. Really, Tina thought, your blood pressure could get so high that the edges of your vision actually shook and wobbled. "You cheated us both, Brian."

"What?" He backed up a step as she stepped forward.

"*You* decided for both of us that I should be protected. You decided that I wasn't woman enough to stand beside my husband."

"No, I—"

"You decided that I was unworthy to be a Marine wife."

"You're twisting all of this around, Tina."

"No, I'm not," she said, and wondered if the hurt and the anger would ever completely drain away. Five years of their lives lost. Five years when they could have been happy, been building a family, been together, living and loving. All gone because Brian Reilly had willed it so. "I've got it straight," she said. "At last. And you were wrong. So wrong. I was *proud* of you. Proud to be the wife of a Marine. Do you think I don't know how important your job is? Well, I do. Sure, it would have been hard, being separated. But I'm strong, Brian. And as long as we loved each other, I could have handled it."

"I know that," he managed to say, "I just didn't want you to have to."

Pain rippled through Tina and she wanted to weep for everything they'd lost. "So to save us from being separated for months at a time," she said, shaking her head sadly, "you separated us permanently. Nice logic. Good choice."

"I did what I thought was best."

"You were wrong."

Brian reached for her, but Tina stepped back quickly. She didn't want him to touch her, to hold her. She didn't want comfort from him. She wanted what he'd never be willing to give her.

She wanted his respect.

And she wanted his love.

"Go away, Brian," she said softly, turning for the kitchen at the back of the house.

"We haven't talked about the baby."

"We'll do that *if* there's a baby," she said, her words drifting back to him as she moved farther away. "For now, I'm through talking to you."

Another week flew past and Brian could still hear Tina's words echoing over and over in his brain. Had he really been so damn wrong? Was it a bad thing to want to protect someone you loved?

He couldn't talk about this with anyone. Not even Liam, because he sure as hell wasn't in the mood to be called a moron again. And he had the distinct feeling that he wouldn't get any sympathy from his family on this one.

Maybe he didn't deserve any sympathy though. Over the past several days, he'd paid closer attention to his friends and their families. Five years ago, he'd been worried about the hardships. But he hadn't really noticed the partnerships.

His friends had good, strong marriages. There was laughter and trust and respect on both sides. If life got hard, they leaned on each other.

Why hadn't he noticed the good along with the bad?

As he waited to find out if Tina really was carrying his child, Brian was forced to rethink decisions made so long ago. And to consider what life might be like if she was pregnant.

If she was, he wanted to be a part of the child's life. That was fact. He couldn't live knowing he had a child out there somewhere who didn't even know him.

But could he be a part of his kid's life and *not* a part of Tina's?

Eleven

A few days later, Tina had deals to manage, even if they were closing three thousand miles away.

Sitting at her grandmother's kitchen table, she cradled the phone on her shoulder and took notes while her assistant talked.

"The Mannerly house is in the final days of escrow," Donna said, her perky voice just a shade too cheerful for Tina. "Are you going to be back in time to walk them through the closing?"

A week, Tina thought. "Yes, I'll be back by then." She'd be home. Back in her neat little condo, with her tidy little world and the occasional date for dinner and a movie and maybe, just maybe, she'd be pregnant.

"That'd be great," Donna cooed. "Suzanna Mannerly called this morning and wanted to thank you for finding her dream house. Turns out she's pregnant. Isn't that great? She's all excited."

"I'm sure," Tina said, and made all the right noises while Donna went on.

"Suzanna said she's going to do up the nursery just the way you suggested when you first showed them the house and—"

Zoning out, Tina only half listened as she remembered, walking through the big old Victorian in Manhattan Beach. Suzanna Mannerly had loved it the minute she'd walked through the front door. And Tina, having been the number one saleswoman in her real estate office for three years running, had known that she had a sale.

But, when she'd taken Suzanna on a tour of the big old house, and proudly showed the woman the nursery that had sheltered generations of children, Tina'd had an epiphany. The very epiphany that had dragged her all the way back to South Carolina to trick her ex-husband into getting her pregnant.

It had suddenly dawned on her that while she'd spent years helping families find homes, build dreams and invest in their futures…she'd neglected her own.

As Suzanna had oohed and aahed over the nursery and its bay window and window seat and conical ceiling, Tina had felt her biological clock erupt into a series of thunderlike tick-tocks. She'd known, just that quickly, just that absolutely, that what she needed wasn't to be found in the hustle and bustle of L.A.—in the thrill of a sale and the quiet cha-ching of money adding up in her savings account.

What she needed, what she *craved*, was a family of her own. Children. A husband.

Now, she had the chance for one and she'd lost the other, one more time.

"Thanks, Donna," Tina interrupted her assistant neatly. As her stomach twisted and her head ached, she realized she just didn't want to talk about other people's dreams coming true anymore. Maybe that made her a small person, but she'd just have to live with it. "Tell Suzanna I'll be back in time to personally hand her the keys to her dream house."

She only wished she could do the same for herself.

As soon as she hung up, the doorbell rang and she grumbled as she pushed up from the chair and stalked to the front door. She was in no mood for company.

Especially if it was Brian. He'd been coming by the house every day, asking if her period had arrived. If she was feeling sick. Telling her that they had to make a decision. Well, her period hadn't arrived yet. And though hope was still lifting inside her, a part of her wanted to tear her own hair out in frustration.

How much harder was it going to be, she wondered, having Brian's child and yet not having Brian?

Oh, she'd been an idiot, no way around it. Thinking she could get pregnant and waltz away again with no twinges of guilt, no regrets. Janet had been so right to advise her against this.

Too bad she hadn't listened.

Because knowing that she still loved Brian was going to make living without him unbearable.

Grabbing the doorknob, she turned it and gave it a vicious tug. She nearly snarled at the woman on the porch, but cut it off when she was greeted by her former mother-in-law's smiling face.

"Maggie."

"Tina, honey," the older woman said, stepping into the house and grinning like a kid at Christmas. "I'm so glad to see you."

Maggie Reilly was short and a little on the plump side. She had Celtic blue eyes as dark as her sons and black hair she kept short and wispy around her pixie-ish face. Her understanding heart and warm nature had made her the perfect mother-in-law and Tina had missed her desperately.

Muffin and Peaches scrambled around her ankles and Maggie spared each of them a quick greeting before straightening up and looking Tina dead in the eye. "I've been on a bus tour of New England with my travel group or I'd have been to see you before this." She cocked her head, folded her arms over her chest and said, "So, have you come back to knock some sense into Brian's head at last?"

Tina laughed and the laugh choked off at the knot in her throat and before she knew it, the tears she'd been holding in for days burst free. Maggie took a step forward, enfolded her in a tight embrace and murmured to her while she cried.

"It's all right now, love. I'll hit him *for* you." Patting her back, Maggie whispered sympathetically. The soft whisper of her native Ireland sang in her voice, giving her speech a rhythm as soothing as a lullaby. "You come with me." Leading Tina back to the kitchen, she sat her down in the closest chair. Turning for the stove, Maggie snatched up the teakettle, filled it at the sink and set it on a burner to heat. "We'll have a little tea, and you can tell me all about my idiot son and what he's done now."

Tina smiled through her tears and blinked her watery vision clear. "Maggie, I've missed you."

"And I've missed you, too." Bustling around a kitchen as familiar to her as her own, Maggie got down cups, teapot and a plate of cookies. "Hasn't Angelina been keeping me up to date on you and what you've been doing out in Hollywood?"

"Not Hollywood," Tina corrected. "Just L.A."

Maggie waved a hand dismissively. "Same difference, if you ask me. All those pretty people and fast parties. I read the papers."

Tina laughed again and this time felt better. It was good. So good, just to sit and be understood.

"And Brian's kept up with you as well," she said, nodding from her position by the stove, as if just by standing there, she could arrange for the water to boil faster.

"He has?"

"'Course he has. Silly man." Maggie shook her head. "Liam's the only one of the four of them that makes a lick of sense to me most times."

"I should have married *him*."

"Well, now," Maggie said with an impish grin, "the church might have been a little cranky about that idea."

Tina tried for a smile, but failed. "Oh, Maggie, I should never have come back here."

"That's where you're wrong, darlin'," the older woman said. "You should never have *left*."

"He didn't want me."

"Nonsense."

"He *divorced* me."

"He *loves* you."

Tina snorted. "He has a strange way of showing it."

"Well, he's a man, isn't he, poor thing." Maggie shook her head, picked up the teakettle and filled the pot on the table. After the kettle was back on the stove, Maggie took a seat opposite Tina and stretched out one hand to her. "Mind you, I love my sons. Every hardheaded, stubborn, prideful one of them. But I'm not the kind of mother who overlooks their faults. I see them as they are, not as I'd wish them to be."

"Meaning?"

"Meaning," Maggie said, "Brian Reilly has been miserable since you two split up."

"Really?"

"Really." Sighing, Maggie gave Tina's hand a pat, then reached for the teapot and poured each of them a steaming cupful. "He's as thick-headed as his father was before him, God rest him." She made a quick sign of the cross, then went on as if she hadn't paused at all. "But the heart of him was gone when you left, Tina. He's never told me why he divorced you. Couldn't pry that out of him, and Liam couldn't either, though he tried, and reported back to me," she added with a smile. "But I can tell you this. He hasn't rested easy since he lost you."

Small comfort, Tina thought sadly. Although, it some weird way, it might have been easier to take if she thought he had moved on. If he'd found someone else to love. If she thought he'd divorced her because *she* wasn't what he'd needed. But how was she supposed to feel knowing that the man she loved had let her go—and still loved her? What kind of peace could she find in that knowledge?

None.

"I don't know how I'm supposed to feel about that, Maggie," she admitted, cupping her hands around the fragile, rose-patterned teacup.

"Do you love him?"

Tina stared at Brian's mother. "That has nothing to do with anything."

"Not an answer at all," Maggie muttered, shaking her head until her silver hoop earrings clashed against her jaw line. "If you two aren't peas in a pod with your concrete skulls."

Tina smiled.

"I'll ask again. Do you still love Brian?"

"I do."

"Well then, that's settled."

Tina snorted. "Maggie, it settles nothing. Love isn't enough. Not for Brian, anyway."

"Faddle." She waved one manicured hand and blew out a dismissive breath. "Love is *everything*, Tina. The only thing that matters."

If she could believe that, maybe it would be enough to make her stay and fight, Tina thought. But if love had been enough, then surely Brian wouldn't have walked away five years ago.

As if she could read her mind—and Tina wouldn't have been the least surprised to find that she could—Maggie leaned in and said, "The question here is, what're you willing to do about it?"

"About what?"

"Brian."

"What can I do?"

Maggie sighed, took a sip of tea, then shook her head. "Tina, an Irishman's head can be as thick as a brick. Sometimes, you need a two by four just to make a dent."

Tina laughed, and though it sounded a little shaky, it was better than crying. "You're telling me to hit him?"

"No, I could do that myself—and will, if you ask me, make no mistake."

She looked so hopeful and eager, Tina had a hard time saying no. But she did.

"Ah, well then, it'll be up to you, dear. You've only to decide if you want him badly enough to fight through that hard knob of a skull of his." She picked up her teacup and leaned back in her chair. "Then you've only to dig in your heels."

"And if I don't?"

"Then, Tina, love, you and my Brian both will have sad, lonely lives when you could have had so much more."

Brian stalked up the shadow-filled driveway and stopped at the gate leading into the backyard. Just beyond that gate, he heard the excited whimpers and scrabbling of tiny nails as his two tiny fans tried to get through the gate to him.

Scowling, he told himself he didn't know which was worse. The way those two dogs had hated him before, or their abject devotion now. Shaking his head, he opened the gate and stepped through, moving cautiously, so as not to stomp on tiny paws. "Okay, okay, I'm here." He bent down and Muffin and Peaches were all over him.

As he petted and stroked quivering little bodies, the back door opened and a slice of lamplight speared into the shadows, spotlighting him.

Tina stood in the doorway, but she didn't look welcoming. No surprise there, of course. Things had been pretty damn cool between them for days now. And damned if he didn't miss talking to her, watching her, hearing her voice.

Every night, his mind tortured him, by replaying images of the hours he'd spent in her arms. With crystal clarity, Brian recalled every touch, every sigh, every whispered word and caress. And he wondered, in those long, sleepless hours, if he'd ever be able to forget. If there would ever come a night when he'd be able to sleep without dreaming of her. Without remembering what he'd lost—not once, but *twice*.

"I've been waiting for you," Tina said and her voice sounded thick, as though she'd been crying.

Brian's heart twisted and he stood up, barely feeling the two little dogs as they jumped at his legs. His hands felt empty, useless, so he stuffed them into his jeans pockets.

She stepped out onto the porch and he studied her. Hair soft and loose around her shoulders, she wore a skinny strapped tank top and a pair of worn denim shorts with frayed hems. Her long, lean legs were bare and the silver toe ring winked at him in the light. He imprinted her image on his brain without even trying.

She would haunt him.

Always.

He swallowed hard. She was right in front of him and yet, she seemed farther away from him than she ever had before. A single thought raced through his mind before he could stop it and he wondered what they would be like now if he hadn't ended their marriage five years ago. He wondered what it would be like to be coming home to her at night. To hear the sounds of kids playing in the house. To know that the lights left burning were for him, to guide him home to warmth.

And he wondered how in the hell he would ever be able to stand returning to a dark, empty apartment night after night for the rest of his life. Suddenly, the years stretched out in front of him and all he saw of the future was a black void, yawning in front of him like a black hole opening up in space. He was a doomed man.

If he'd stayed married to her, he would have sentenced her to a life of hardship. By setting her free, he'd sentenced himself to a lifetime of emptiness.

But that was a decision he'd made long ago and now he just had to live with it. Blowing out a breath, he squared his shoulders, lifted his chin and asked the question he'd put to her every day for the last week or so.

"Everything all right? You feeling okay?"

"I'm fine."

He nodded, and knowing she didn't want him around, turned for the gate. He had one hand on the worn, weather-beaten wood when her voice stopped him again.

"I'm fine. But there's no baby."

His hand clenched on the top of the gate and his grip was so tight, he wouldn't have been surprised to feel the wood snap clean off. His insides twisted and a laser shot of pain sliced him in two. Somehow though, he managed to stay upright. Swiveling his head, he looked at her. "You're sure?"

"My period started this afternoon," she said and her voice sounded…*hollow*. "So you don't have to worry anymore. You're in the clear."

Was he? He would always wonder about that.

No baby.

There'd never been a baby.

So why then, did he suddenly feel like he was in

mourning? Why did the pain tighten like a vise around his heart and twist in his guts? Why the sorrow? The regret?

Wasn't this what he'd been hoping for?

Wasn't this for the best?

And if it *was* for the best, shouldn't he be feeling happy? Instead, he was feeling as though the earth had opened up beneath him and he was tottering on the lip of a rocky chasm.

Deliberately, he forced himself to loosen his grip on the old gate. "I don't know what I should say," he admitted quietly.

"There's nothing *to* say, Brian," Tina said softly. "Not anymore."

Then she snapped her fingers and the dogs reluctantly left him, scampering up the steps and through the open doorway into the lamplit house. Tina stared at him for a long minute and looked as though she was going to speak again. But she changed her mind and quietly closed the door.

That spear of light was gone.

The promise of warmth was shut off.

And Brian was alone.

In the dark.

Twelve

By noon the next day, Angelina Coretti was home, greeting her nearly hysterically-glad-to-see-her dogs, and Tina was packing.

"You should stay," the older woman said to her granddaughter, trying to look stern as she cradled first one tiny dog and then the other, giving each of them equal attention.

"I can't, Nana," Tina said as she tossed shorts and T-shirts into the oversized, navy blue suitcase. "I just can't stay."

Angelina clucked her tongue, set Muffin down on the floor, then walked to her granddaughter. Laying one hand on her arm, she waited until Tina was looking at her to speak again. "Is it Brian?"

It was *always* Brian, Tina thought, diving into the pool of misery that lay deep in the bottom of her heart. All night, she'd been torn by the knowledge that she had to leave.

Talking to Maggie hadn't helped. If anything, it had only made Tina feel worse. Knowing that Brian had been miserable without her was small consolation. If Tina'd been able to convince herself that he'd divorced her because he wanted someone else, it would have been hard to swallow, but she'd eventually have succeeded. But knowing that the damn man hadn't wanted anyone but her and had *still* divorced her only made the whole situation more heartbreaking.

How could she possibly argue with a man so willing to walk away from love? From what they'd had? From what they might have had?

Angelina sighed and sat down on the edge of the bed. Reaching into the suitcase, she pulled out one of Tina's shirts and absently folded it as she spoke. "I'd hoped that the two of you would find a way back to each other during these weeks."

"Nana." Tina stopped what she was doing and stared at her grandmother. Angelina Coretti was tall and slim. Her silver hair was still long and thick and she wore it in a braided knot at the back of her head. Her features were lined in patterns created by years of smiling and her dark brown eyes were filled with the warm understanding that Tina had grown up with.

The older woman shrugged and reached for another shirt to fold. "Do you think I don't know why you never visit except when you know Brian will be gone?" she asked with a shake of her head. "Did you think I couldn't tell that you still love him?"

Sighing, Tina dropped her makeup bag into the suitcase, then took a seat beside her grandmother. "Never could put one over on you, could I?"

"Surprising that you still try." Angelina patted her hand, then gave it a squeeze. "Brian was the one for you," she said softly. "Right from the first. And it was the same for him."

"Doesn't matter," Tina said and fought the rising pain within. No point in worrying her grandmother. There'd be plenty of time for tears, for regrets, once she got home.

"Of course it matters," Angelina snapped. "It's the only thing that *does* matter. I thought you knew better than that."

Tina smiled grimly. "Even if I do know better, Brian doesn't. And I can't make a marriage all on my own, Nana."

"You're both too stubborn, you know." Angelina huffed out a disgusted breath.

"That's what Maggie said yesterday."

"Smart woman."

"I'll miss you," Tina said, turning her hand over so she could link fingers with her grandmother.

"Oh, honey, I'll miss you, too." Angelina turned slightly on the bed. "Why don't you stay?" she urged. "Don't give up so easily. Stay here where you belong. This is your *home,* Tina."

Home.

She was right. Baywater was home. Here, there was Nana and Maggie and Liam and the slower life-style Tina'd forgotten how much she loved. Here there were warm breezes and magnolia trees and the scent of jasmine flavoring every breath. Here, there were neighbors and the streets she'd grown up on. There were people who knew her, loved her.

Here, there was Brian.

And that's why she couldn't stay.

Everything she'd come home for was gone. The hope for a baby, the yearning for Brian. It had all dissolved like a piece of sugar in the rain. Her wishes, her dreams, were puddled around her.

She needed to get away—she wouldn't think of it as *running*—from the death of those hopes. She needed to see everything that had happened recently more clearly. And for that she needed distance.

Three thousand miles might be enough.

"I can't," Tina said and heard the regret in her own voice. "I hope you understand, Nana. But even if you don't, I have to go."

Her grandmother sighed, gave Tina's hand another pat, then stood up and laid a pair of pale green shorts on top of the clothes in the suitcase. "I understand, honey. Wish I didn't, but I do."

"Thanks for that."

Nodding, Angelina shot her a look from the corner of her eye. "Are you going to at least say goodbye to Brian?"

"No." Tina stood up, too, and reached for another shirt to throw into the bag.

"Too scared?"

She sighed. "Too tired."

Brian left the base early, but he didn't go home.

He still wasn't ready yet to face Tina.

If that was cowardly, then he'd have to suck it up.

Instead, he went to the Lighthouse to meet his brothers. Now, he was trying to remember why it had seemed like a good idea at the time.

"You're letting her go, *again?*" Connor snorted, leaned back in the booth and took a long swig of his beer.

"I'm not *letting* her do anything," Brian pointed out in his own defense. "Tina goes where she wants, does what she wants."

"Uh-huh," Aidan said with a smirk at Connor. "And she's leaving because…?"

"How the hell do I know?" Brian countered, but

he *did* know. He knew all too well why Tina was leaving. Because there was no baby. No future. With him. And that was a good thing. She was better off without him. And God knew, they were better off without having made a child they'd have to figure out a long-distance way to share.

He rubbed the center of his chest when the ache came again. He was almost used to the nagging pain now. It came whenever he remembered that there was no baby. That Tina was leaving. That he'd never see her again once Angelina came home.

Scowling, he told himself that he'd gotten used to Tina's absence five years ago, he'd get used to it again. With that thought in mind, he signaled the waitress for another beer.

"You do know though, don't you, Brian?" Liam asked, jabbing him in the ribs with an elbow.

Turning that fierce frown on his brother, he snapped, "If you're looking for a confession here, I suggest you head back to your flock."

"Ooh," Connor said, grinning. "Touchy."

"Pitiful," Aidan said. "Just pitiful. Man can't even admit it to himself."

"Admit what?" Brian thanked the waitress for the fresh, icy cold beer she'd brought him and took a long pull at it. Life would have been much simpler, he thought briefly, if he'd been an only child.

"That you love her, you moron," Liam said softly.

Brian's breath hitched in his chest and it felt as though a cold hand were fisting around his heart. *Love.* What was it about that one little word that could bring a man to his knees? What was it that made a man so reluctant to look at that word honestly? Objectively?

His gaze shifted around the restaurant. He took it all in. The same, familiar faces that he usually saw there at this time of day. The same families. The same children, turning to their parents. The same couples, huddled together in booths, sharing whispered conversations and unspoken promises.

And it suddenly hit him that there wasn't a damn thing objective about love.

You either felt it or you didn't.

Wanted it or ran from it.

Appreciated it or threw it away.

Damn it.

Brian slid a glance at his older brother. "You know, I'm getting really tired of you calling me names."

"Then stop being stupid."

"Do they teach you those comforting little sayings in the seminary?" Brian wondered aloud.

"Shut up," Connor said and snickered when Brian sent him a you-are-dead-meat glare. "If you think you worry me, you're wrong."

"Why am I here?" Brian asked no one in particular.

"Because you're too dumb to admit you'd rather be with Tina," Connor said.

"You already lost the bet, Bri." Aidan picked a tortilla chip out of the basket in the middle of the table and crunched down on it. "What's holding you back?"

"This is not about the bet."

"Then what?" Liam prodded.

"It's about being fair," Brian argued.

"To who?" Connor demanded.

"To Tina." Brian leaned in over the table, and swept his gaze across his brothers' faces, one after the other. "Being a Marine wife is hard. Harder than any other job out there and you guys know it."

"What's your point?" Aidan asked.

"I want Tina to have better," Brian snapped. "She deserves better."

"Better than loving and being loved?" Liam asked.

Brian slumped back against the booth seat and cradled his beer between his palms. Shaking his head, he muttered stubbornly, "She deserves better."

Connor snorted.

Aidan opened his mouth to speak.

Liam held up one hand to silence him and then looked at Brian. "She deserves the chance to decide for herself," he said quietly. "She deserves to have the man she loves respect her enough to give her a *choice*."

"You don't underst—"

Liam cut him off. "She knew when she married you that you were a Marine. She grew up in a military town. She knows what being a military wife means. And she *chose* to love you. To marry you."

Brian heard the words and let them sink in. As he did, he felt a flicker of light shimmer in the darkness within and hope bubbled up inside him. Images of Tina raced through his mind, one after the other. Her eyes flashing, her mouth curving, her arms encircling him. He heard her laugh again, felt the soft sigh of her breath on his cheek and relived the sensation of her turning to him in her sleep.

And he knew.

Damn it, he'd always known.

Hard or not, life wasn't worth living without her.

"I gotta go," he muttered, reaching for his wallet and tearing a couple of bills out. He tossed them onto the table and slid out of the booth. Staring down at his brothers, he gave them a quick grin and said, "Gotta talk to Tina."

"Better hurry," Connor said, lifting his beer in a half-assed salute.

"Yeah," Aidan added, "before she remembers what a jerk you are."

As Brian darted between the crowded tables, the three remaining Reilly brothers clinked their beer bottles together and smiled.

* * *

Three days back in California and Tina knew what she had to do. Actually, to be honest, she'd known before she flew back to the land of perpetual sun and smog.

But she'd had to come here to be positive.

Now she was.

Smiling to herself, she shuffled the papers on her desk, straightened them up and set them in the file marked "urgent." Janet would take care of it all. She knew Tina's cases as well as or better than she did herself.

Everything would be fine.

And now, so would she.

"Are you sure about this?" Janet rubbed her swollen belly as if rubbing a good luck charm. "I mean, you just got back, maybe you should take more time and—"

Tina shot her a quick grin and shook her head. She would miss Janet, but they'd keep in touch. Telephone calls, e-mail, visits, somehow, someway, they'd do it.

"Trust me on this," Tina said. "I've already had five years. I've thought this through and it's what I have to do."

Janet sighed. "Okay, but it's not going to be the same around here without you."

"Thanks." Tina came around her cluttered desk and hugged her friend tightly. "I'll miss you, too."

* * *

Brian hated L.A.

Always had.

He'd been stationed at Pendleton for a couple of years once and the crowds had chewed at him. Just too damn many people. And they all seemed to be on the freeway at the same time.

While he sat in traffic, his brain kicked into high gear, as if trying to make up for the standstill by revving at top speed.

He'd left the restaurant, determined to talk to Tina. To apologize. To do whatever he had to do to make her listen. To make her know that he loved her. Always had. Always would. He'd finally gotten it through his thick head that love wasn't something fragile to be protected. It was something strong, something to lean on when things got rough. And there was nobody stronger than Tina.

He'd just been so determined to take care of her, that he hadn't realized that a marriage was about taking care of each other.

But when he got home, he'd found Angelina, back from Italy and just mad enough at him to tell him that Tina had left for L.A.

Gone.

Just like that.

With no word.

No warning.

But then, he hadn't really deserved one, had he? he thought now. Remembering the blind panic that had shot through him, he nearly strangled on it. He'd tried to catch her at the airport but her flight had already left by the time he got there.

He could have called her, but he knew that what he had to say couldn't be said on a phone. He had to be standing in front of her, so she could see his eyes, so he could reach out for her and hold on if she decided to make this harder than it had to be.

So, he'd spent the next two days wangling a brief leave and then talking his way onto a transport plane headed to Camp Pendleton. Now, his rental car was overheating and he was stuck in traffic next to a teenager in a black truck with a stereo system loud enough to reach Mars.

And all he could think was, he hoped he hadn't waited too long. Hoped he wasn't too late.

Tina looked around her office, exhaled deeply and smiled to herself. Finished. It was done and she was ready.

More than ready, she told herself, she was anxious to get started.

"Tina!"

She jolted and spun around, one hand reaching for the base of her throat. "Brian?"

"Damn it," he shouted again, his voice carrying

from the main office with no trouble at all, "I'm here to see Tina Coretti, and I'm not leaving until I do."

Heart pounding, brain reeling, Tina hurried through the open doorway leading from her office to the real estate business's main room. She spotted him easily. A tall, gorgeous, totally built Marine, surrounded by men who suddenly looked much smaller in comparison, was hard to miss.

He saw her instantly and his features shifted from angry frustration to desperation. "Tina, tell these yahoos who I am."

"It's okay," she called out and ignored the questioning looks being tossed her way. "He's my ex-husband."

Brian pushed through the rest of the people standing between him and Tina and headed for her.

"Oh, wow," Janet said from directly beside her and Tina was forced to agree.

Brian in uniform was something to see. His chest was broad and the medals pinned to his left breast glittered in the sunlight streaming through the bank of floor to ceiling windows. His blue eyes were focused on Tina and his jaw was locked tight.

He stopped just a foot from her and took a long deep breath before blurting, "You left without telling me."

"What?" she asked and nearly shook her head as if to clear it.

"You heard me," he said and his voice boomed out

around them. "I went to Angelina's to talk to you and you were gone."

"You knew I wasn't staying," she said and shot a quick look at the interested faces turned toward them.

"Yeah." He shoved one hand along the side of his head then let his hand drop. "But I want you to stay."

"Brian—"

"I came to take you home," he said, not letting her get more than that one word out.

Tina felt the earth shift beneath her and decided she liked it. "You did?"

"I can't live without you, Tina. Not anymore. Not one more day." He reached for her, dropping both hands onto her shoulders and squeezing, as if holding her in place should she decide to make a run for it.

But Tina wasn't going anywhere.

"You can't?" she asked, wanting to hear it all. Hear everything she'd waited five long years for.

"I thought I was doing the right thing before," he said and at last his voice dropped until it was as if just the two of them were in the room. "When I let you go. Being a Marine wife is hard. A tough job not everyone can do."

"I could have," she said, needing him to know that he'd made a mistake.

"I know that now," he agreed. "You're plenty tough enough," he added, then lifted one hand to stroke her cheek. "Tougher than me, because you were able to leave and I couldn't let you."

Tears rushed up from her heart, filled her throat and blurred her eyes. "Not so tough," she said, catching his hand with hers and holding on. "It killed me to leave."

"Then come home," he said, softer now, more intimately. "Come home with me, Tina. Love me. Let me love you. I've always loved you, Tina. Always will love you."

"Brian…"

He pulled her close, wrapping his arms around her until all Tina could feel was him. His heart pounded and she felt the thud of it echo inside her.

"Make babies with me, Tina," he whispered, his breath a hush on her ear. "Make lots of babies with me."

Joy rippled through her, one wave after another, like circles on the surface of a lake after a pebble had been tossed in. She held on to him, holding him as tightly as she could and whispered for him alone. "I love you, Brian Reilly. Always have. Always will. I was always proud to be a Marine wife. And even prouder to be *your* wife."

Relief crashed through him like storm surf and left his legs shaky. Brian had never felt better in his life. Pulling her back so that he could look into her beautiful, teary eyes, he said, "So then. How fast do you think we can move you back to South Carolina?"

"Does tomorrow work for you?"

Stunned, Brian just stared at her. "Huh?"

Laughing, Tina grabbed his hand and ignoring everyone else, dragged him down the short hall to her office and closed the door behind them. Then she flung herself at him, wrapping her arms around his neck and grinning up into his face.

"I sold my half of the business to my partner," she said. "Movers are coming tomorrow to pack up my stuff."

"You—but—how—" He sounded like an idiot and he was so damn happy, he didn't care.

Shaking her head, Tina leaned in and planted a long, deep kiss on him before pulling back again. "I decided two days ago that I couldn't stay here—that I couldn't live without you."

His arms tightened around her and his heart gave a lurch that jolted him.

"I was going home to you, you big dummy," Tina said, smiling. "To make you love me. To make you see that we belong together."

"Baby," he said, pausing for another soul-searing kiss, "I'm convinced."

And when they finally came up for air again, Brian gave her a tight squeeze and warned, "You realize you're marrying a man who's going to have to be seen in a hula skirt and a coconut bra."

"I'll bring a camera," she said on a teary laugh.

"And I'll even pose for you," Brian told her, "because I've never been happier about losing a bet."

* * * * *

Don't miss the next installment of the
THREE-WAY WAGER *series.*
WHATEVER REILLY WANTS
…is available
in June
from Silhouette Desire.

If you enjoyed what you just read,
then we've got an offer you can't resist!

Take 2 bestselling love stories FREE!

Plus get a FREE surprise gift!

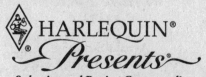

COMING NEXT MONTH

#1657 ESTATE AFFAIR—Sara Orwig
Dynasties: The Ashtons
Eli Ashton couldn't resist one night of passion with Lara Hunter, the maid at Ashton Estates. Horrified that she had fallen into bed with such a powerful man, Lara fled the scene, leaving Eli wanting more. Could he convince Lara that their estate affair was the stuff fairy tales were made of?

#1658 WHATEVER REILLY WANTS…—Maureen Child
Three-Way Wager
All Connor Reilly had to do to win his no-sex-for-ninety-days bet was spend time with the one woman who wouldn't tempt him. Yet Emma Jacobsen had other plans, plans that involved a *very* short skirt and a change in attitude. Emma's transformation had Connor forgetting about his wager—but was what they had strong enough to last longer than ninety days?

#1659 SECRETS OF PATERNITY—Susan Crosby
Behind Closed Doors
Caryn Brenley and P.I. James Paladin had a son without ever meeting face-to-face *or* skin-to-skin. When Caryn learned James was her child's sperm donor, she reluctantly agreed to let father and son meet. James jumped at the opportunity, but pretty soon he wanted to get close to Caryn—the natural way.

#1660 SCANDALOUS PASSION—Emilie Rose
Phoebe Drew feared intimate photos of her and her first love, Carter Jones, would jeopardize her grandfather's political career. So she went to Carter for help in finding them. But digging up the past also uncovered long-hidden passion, leaving Phoebe to wonder if falling for Carter again would prove to be her most scandalous decision.

#1661 THE SULTAN'S BED—Laura Wright
Sultan Zayad Al-Nayhal came to California to find his sister, but instead ended up spending time with her roommate, Mariah Kennedy. Mariah trusted no man—especially tall, dark and gorgeous ones. True, Zayad possessed all of these qualities, but he was ready to plead a personal case that even this savvy lawyer couldn't resist.

#1662 BLAME IT ON THE BLACKOUT—Heidi Betts
When a blackout brought their elevator to a screeching halt, personal assistant Lucy Grainger and her sinfully handsome boss, Peter Reynolds, gave in to unbridled passion. When the lights kicked back in, so did denial of their mutual attraction. Yet Peter found that his dreams of corporate success were suddenly being fogged by dreams of Lucy….

SDCNM0505